MIND WARS

MIND WARS

A gripping tale of redemption, forgiveness, and the enduring bonds forged in the crucible of war, a story that reflects on the tragic price veterans continue to pay for our freedom.

ROGER GERALD SCOTT

Contents

ADJUSTMENT

RECONSTRUCTION

REALITY

For those who made the ultimate sacrifice and those
who continue to fight.

Visit: https://mindwarsbook.com/
Proofreading by The Pro Book Editor
eBook ISBN: 978-82-693205-1-0
paperback ISBN: 978-82-693205-0-3

1. Main category—FICTION / Historical / General
2. Other categories—FICTION / War & Military
    First Edition

Acknowledgements

This book would not have been possible without certain people. A big thanks to Aud, Yvonne, Christian, Aleksander, Trine, Gerd, Tim Sear, Graeme Austin, Jane Price, and Debra Hartmann.

I would also like to thank the many veterans and islanders who assisted me along the way. In no particular order: Dave (Charlie) Brown, John Howard, Tony Rafferty, Kevin J Porter, Robert Lawrence, Simon Bird, Tony Banks, and Lisa Watson.

A special mention to Ricky Strange for his unwavering and fantastic support throughout the eight-year project.

Finally, I would like to thank Mike Hall, a Falklands veteran who went out of his way to help me at the beginning of this project. Without him, this book would never have made it.

DENIAL

Chapter 1

It wasn't Scottish ale or companionship that lured Frank Drysdale to the King's Arms Pub—it was solitude. Mornings were always quiet in the small seaside town of Tayport, Scotland, and with nobody around to disturb him, Frank could take his pint and head outside to the beer garden. It was a ritual he had missed during the recent lockdown, sitting at the same wooden table in the corner of the garden, defiantly enduring the Scottish weather as he soaked in the nearby views of the Tentsmuir National Nature Reserve, Broughty Castle, the forested dunes, and the River Tay. He loved how the strong wind soothed his mind and the sea air calmed him. His heart rate slowed, the muscles relaxed, and his breathing became slower. For a short while, he was able to forget his troubles.

But today as he sat down, he felt no peace. Even out here in the fresh Scottish air, there was no escaping his nightmares. He could still smell the phosphorus and still hear the artillery and high-pitched screams of men as his mother taunted him. To make things worse, a thick fog obscured his view and the wind passed unchallenged through his thick winter jacket, making him feel unusually cold. Even his beer tasted bitter and metallic, like someone had poisoned it.

Dispirited, he picked up his pint glass and quickly poured half the Scottish ale down his throat. As he was about to place it back down on the table, he suddenly became aware that he was no longer alone. Someone had crept into the garden from behind him, and he was about to turn around when a loud bang rang out. It was a sound he recognised straight away—the distinct sound of gunfire. A pistol shot.

A feeling of dizziness quickly came over him and, losing his balance, he fell off the wooden bench and onto the pavement. There was a big smashing sound as the pint glass he was holding broke into hundreds of little pieces around him, letting the remains of his beer spill across the nearby grass.

As he lay on his back staring up at the sky, he could feel his consciousness begin to ebb away from him. Unable to move, he realised he was dying and a wave of sadness overwhelmed him. All he could think about was a promise he had made many years ago. A promise made to a good friend. A promise he would now never keep. Desperate, he tried to shout "Kevin," but only a whisper came, drowned out by a gust of wind. His face turned an ashen white as his consciousness left him.

Chapter 2

Kevin Turner was not used to waking up to silence. Usually, his mornings began by arguing with the wife before getting his four-year-old daughter clothed and fed, then dropping her off at the nursery on his way to work. Today, his third day as a separated man in a rented flat, there was no noise at all, only an eerie silence.

Having taken the week off work, he had hoped a few quiet mornings alone might clear his mind, but guilty thoughts crept in about how his separation was going to affect his daughter and what would happen to the friends and family they had shared for the last seven years. Frustrated at his inability to relax, he got out of bed.

Picking up his mobile phone from the nearby chair, he noticed the same unknown number had called him several times. On closer examination, he saw there was a text message from the same number.

"George Stafford here. Please call me. Urgent."

The name was immediately familiar. George was the landlord of the King's Arms Pub in Tayport, a few hundred yards down the road from where he had grown up. Even though it had been twenty years since he'd moved to Dundee, he remembered the man well. George's nickname, "Gorilla," conjured up an image of a well-built man with a huge muscular frame. He could still hear the man's gravelly voice and remember his habit of calling everyone "mate" whether they were or not. It had been a long time since they'd spoken, and curious as to why he had called, Kevin rang back.

As soon as George answered, it quickly became apparent this was not a social call. "It's Frank, mate," he mumbled.

"Frank?" Kevin replied, surprised at the mention of his adoptive father. When Kevin's real parents died in 1982, it was Frank, his dad's best friend, who had come to the rescue, bringing him up with the help of Frank's mother, Auntie Kay, as she was affectionately known. Now he had a horrible feeling George was about to tell him Frank was dead. "What's happened?" he said, bracing himself for the worst.

"This morning he fainted in my beer garden."

"Fainted?" Kevin replied.

"Yeah."

"So...you mean he's okay?" Kevin asked, relieved but confused.

"Well, okay is not the word I would use, mate," George replied, sounding disgusted that Kevin wasn't as appalled as he was. "This morning I was going outside to empty some ashtrays in the beer garden, but I forgot to close the door and it slammed behind me. Next thing I know, I see the daft sod's collapsed on the bloody pavement!"

Kevin remained silent, unwilling to interrupt and make George even more angry.

"He's been behaving very strange lately, mate. He doesn't talk to anyone anymore, drinks too much. For a second, I thought he'd had a heart attack. I nearly called an ambulance, but he came 'round. But do you know what happened then? Do you know what he told me?"

Hearing the disgust in his voice, Kevin decided against guessing.

"He said someone had *shot* him, Kevin! Shot him! For Christ's sake, he's losing it, mate."

Unsure what George wanted him to do about it, Kevin asked, "Where is he now, still in the pub?"

"I sent him home."

"Okay," Kevin said, still unsure how to respond. He was sure it was just Frank drinking too much, nothing more. The pandemic lockdown hadn't been easy for anyone, and he knew Frank had been depressed after his mother's death six months earlier.

"Look, mate, do me a favour. Just give him a call, talk some sense into him?" George said, his desperate voice rising in volume.

Kevin sighed. George seemed to have forgotten he and his foster parent had been estranged for years. He had always found talking to Frank difficult, like there had always been an unspoken tension between them. He could not ever recall having a meaningful chat with Frank before, so what would be the point now? Besides, at this moment in time, he had other more pressing problems to consider, like trying to get his own life back on track after his recent separation. Now that it was clear Frank wasn't a corpse needing to be picked up off the pub garden, he was even more reluctant to interfere.

"I'll see what I can do, George," Kevin lied, then thanked him for calling and hung up.

As he made himself a cup of coffee and sat down to watch the television, he found himself unable to forget the phone call. What George had told him about fainting and gunshots seemed so absurd, and why had the guy gone out of his way to find his number and call him? Something wasn't right.

What if Frank really was ill?

It was just a phone call, he reminded himself as he stared at his mobile. He dialled Frank's mobile number and waited.

Chapter 3

Frank lay down on his sofa and opened a can of beer. As he quickly drank half of the contents, he noticed the living room was in the same state it had been all week. Despite leaving the house an hour ago to walk to the pub, the television was still on and the curtains and windows still open. Nobody had cleaned up the mess of beer bottles and old newspapers. The wooden floor was still covered with a thin layer of dust, making it look like a closed museum. Normally, it would have been a depressing reminder that his dead mother was no longer around to clear up after him, but today, he had more important things to think about and the cluttered state of the house didn't bother him.

As he stared blankly at the television, he continued to mull over the earlier events. He could have sworn someone had crept into the pub garden from behind and shot him with a pistol. He clearly remembered hearing the distinct and familiar bang of the gunshot and wondering who wished him dead. He also recalled the regret that a promise he had made years earlier to a close friend would remain unkept.

But he had not died, only fainted. Regaining consciousness, he had looked up and seen a worried looking George looming over him. Embarrassed and confused, he had grabbed the landlord's arm, hoisted himself up and, after convincing George he was okay, staggered back home.

His thoughts were interrupted by a loud rattling sound in his kitchen. Despite being on silent, his mobile phone was vibrating on the wooden table. He hated the disturbance of mobile phones and, angry at himself for forgetting to turn it off earlier, he got up and walked into the kitchen to see who was calling.

As he picked up his mobile, he stared at the screen in disbelief. *Kevin Turner?* What the hell did he want? He hadn't seen or spoken to him for months!

Right now, he was the last person in the world he wanted to talk to. Furious at the intrusion, he turned off the phone, grabbed another beer from the fridge, and rushed back to the sofa.

The moment he sat down again, he was hit by a wave of tiredness. Straight away, his body tensed up in fear. For the last few months, he had been experiencing very unpleasant nightmares. Chronic, disturbing dreams that made him too scared to sleep.

It had only been four of five hours since he last slept, but he could feel his bones getting heavier and his senses overwhelming him. Sleep was slowly creeping up on him, and there was nothing he could do. Exhausted, he leaned back against the headrest of the sofa and closed his eyes.

As he fell into a deep sleep, his nightmare began. It was always the same dream, on a battlefield thousands of miles away from home, lying in wet mud as he took cover behind a small rock. Even though it was night, the sky was ablaze with tracers of red and green and flashes of white phosphorus. In front of him, up the gradual rocky incline less than a thousand yards away, the enemy bombarded his regiment with artillery and mortars. As the wet ground shook from the heavy weaponry, he could hear soldiers nearby shouting and screaming.

But it wasn't the sights and sounds of battle that held his attention. It was the lifeless enemy soldier lying on the ground face up a few yards away, to his right. As he stared at the face, he saw the eyes flickering open and shut at high speed and its mouth moving to say something. Curious, he crawled a little closer and listened.

"Why, Frankie? Why?" it whispered to him, the words inexplicably clear amidst the noise around him.

He froze as he recognised the voice of his mother, unable to understand what she was doing on this bleak battlefield so far from home.

"Why, Frankie? Why?" she whispered again.

Before he had time to reply, there was a big white flash and a loud scream followed by an explosion that covered him in a red mist.

This was always the moment he woke up to the sound of his own screams. Opening his eyes, he was overcome with panic and nausea as he struggled to breathe. His clothes were drenched in sweat and every inch of his body pricked by pins and needles. He had moved so much while asleep that his feet were now on the opposite side of the sofa and his head hung over the edge, inches from the floor. Falling to the floor, he ran to the bathroom to be sick.

It took ten minutes before he felt secure enough to venture out of the bathroom. Even as he did, the stench of gunpowder and death still lingered in the air—the unmistakeable smell of burning gorse mingled with the pungent odour of blood.

He had to get out of this house. *Now.*

He looked at his watch and ran to the front door. At this time of the day, there was only one place he could go.

Chapter 4

As Kevin drove across the Tay Road Bridge and onto the B946, George's angry words were still ringing in his ears.

"For Christ's sake, he's back," George had shouted into the phone minutes earlier.

At first, he'd felt George's anger was unfair. He had called Frank as requested. It wasn't his fault that the guy had not picked up the phone, but it quickly became clear the situation was more serious than Kevin had believed.

"Please," George had pleaded, breathlessly explaining how Frank had shown up at the pub again, this time looking even more fragile. "He's dying, mate," he had then shouted in a desperate tone.

"Okay, I'm on my way now," Kevin had replied, at once hanging up and running to the front door, picking up his car keys on the way.

The nearer he got to Tayport, the more George's words unnerved him. The guy was not even sixty years old, so "dying" felt like an inappropriate description. As far as Kevin could recall, Frank had never been ill or in hospital, his only medical problem had been some childhood accident that left him with a permanent stiff right shoulder, making lifting heavy objects difficult. He knew Frank's mother's death had hit him hard. Apart from the time he got married and moved out, he had spent almost his whole life living with his mother, in the same house in Tayport. Auntie Kay had spent most of her life looking after her only son, spoiling him, cooking his food and washing his clothes. But then, a few months ago, at the age of 76, she had collapsed at home with heart failure. It had been a huge shock for Frank. Alone and with nobody to look after him, he struggled to adjust.

However, now that George had convinced him Frank was ill, Kevin was beginning to regret their estranged relationship over the years. He still found it hard to feel he was to blame when Frank had resisted all his efforts to make their association more pleasant. Frank never answered the phone when he called. He hadn't come to Kevin's wedding despite being invited and still hadn't met Kevin's daughter, Rose. So why was he driving over to see him now? Yet the call this morning had made him emotional, and he wasn't sure why. Perhaps it was the fact that Frank was a war veteran, someone who deserved better than to spend his last years alone. Maybe it was because, despite everything, Kevin knew he had a lot to thank Frank for. His parents had died when he was only a few months old, and Frank had saved him from foster care. Thanks to Auntie Kay, it had been a good childhood and he had never forgotten the sacrifice Frank made by adopting him. Whatever problems had passed between them over the years, they now seemed petty. Frank needed him. He had to try.

Arriving at the King's Arms Pub, Kevin parked his car and put on his mask. Even though he had not been there for years, the old Victorian pub located on a quiet back street just outside the town had not changed. It still had the weather-beaten white walls he remembered so well from his youth when he had been sent by Auntie Kay to pick Frank up and get him home.

The pub was quiet as he made his way inside. Straight ahead, behind the bar, he spotted George, who must have seen Kevin coming as two beers were already waiting for him on the bar.

"Hi, Kev. Thanks for coming. I appreciate it," George said as Kevin approached.

Even with the mask on, he noticed George had aged a lot, though he still had the same expressionless face. He could have witnessed a hundred people being killed and still have the same look. He was a man who seemed to have spent his whole life behind this very bar, and Kevin could only imagine all the crazy things he had witnessed over the years. He reached for his wallet, but George waved his hand to brush the formality away.

"No, mate, I appreciate you came. On the house," he said as he winked at Kevin, as if making it clear that the beers would double as a peace offering to make Frank more receptive to his arrival.

"When was the last time you saw him, Kev? Was it a while ago?" George asked.

"Well, I saw him briefly about six months ago, at the funeral."

"Oh, I see. It was just that, Kev, when he fainted this morning, well, it was weird, mate. He..." George stopped, seeming embarrassed to say more.

"He what, George?"

"Well, he was lying with his back on the grass, soaked in beer, clutching his arm as if he had been shot. As I got down on my knees to check if he was breathing, I heard he was whispering your name."

"Whispering *my* name? Are you sure?" Kevin almost shouted. That Frank would now be whispering Kevin's name as he fainted seemed so unlikely. Perhaps George's hearing was deserting him.

"Thought you should know. Has anything happened recently?"

"Nothing at all," Kevin said softly, noticing a customer approaching the bar from his right, about to distract George's attention. Eager to get on with task ahead, he said his thanks and picked up the two pints of beer. He made his way across the dirty stone floor, past the toilets, and headed for the door to the beer garden.

As he put his elbow on the door handle, Kevin suddenly felt very alone. He wondered nervously what sort of Frank he would be confronted with today. Frank had always been impatient, with a short temper, and Kevin had never really shaken off the feeling of disapproval. Feeling brave, he pushed open the back door and walked up the small stone steps into the garden.

Even without looking up, he knew exactly where Frank was sitting. He always sat at the same light green, circular wooden bench in the far-left corner. Even if the garden had been full of customers, Kevin still would have spotted him for he was a tall, thin man, the over lanky kind who always stood out in a crowd because of their unusual height. As he approached, he saw a preoccupied Frank huddled up at the bench, looking out over the distant bay, oblivious to Kevin's presence. It was only when he sat down opposite him and made a coughing noise that Frank finally turned around.

Kevin was horrified by the sight that greeted him. George had been right after all, Frank did look like death. The dark bags under his eyes seemed to have doubled in size since he'd last seen him, as if he hadn't slept for weeks. Not only had the man lost a lot of weight but his earlier confidence and swagger had gone, like someone had crept up behind him and stabbed him in the back. But it was the eyes staring back at him that worried Kevin the most. Empty, soulless, blank eyes, like there was nobody inside.

Frank's eyes seemed to cloud over in a mixture of shock and surprise. He blinked furiously, as though trying hard to scramble a memory that might help him identify who this person was. It was a look Kevin had seen many times before but never so intense. Not even the beer glass Kevin pushed toward him seemed to register.

There followed an awkward silence, but eventually, much to Kevin's relief, Frank's face lit up in recognition. "Kev," he said, almost with a soft tone of disbelief.

Or was it disgust, Kevin wondered. "Hi, Frank," he said, relieved that the man at least recognised him.

"What are you doing here?" Frank asked suspiciously.

"I was just driving past and thought I would pop in," Kevin replied, running his left hand through his hair nervously.

As they commenced small chat, Kevin was reminded how little had changed. Frank seemed unable to relax when he was around, unable to look at Kevin for long, and, in the rare moments when he spoke more than a few mono-syllables, he stumbled with his words. Conversation was, as it had always been, frustrating and challenging work. What annoyed Kevin most was that this behaviour seemed to be exclusively reserved for him. He wasn't like this with other people. With others, he had no trouble cracking jokes, but for Kevin, the topic of conversation was the same as it had been thirty years ago—either about George and his outrageous beer prices or disdain for the yuppy university students who invaded the pub at every opportunity. Ill or not, it was hard for Kevin not to let all the bitterness come back. Had Frank forgotten that Kevin had a four-year-old daughter? Did he know Kevin was separated? Did he even care?

Kevin didn't take long to drink his beer. Ready to leave, there was no way he wanted to prolong this circus. Coming here had been uncomfortable, emotionally draining, and besides, it wasn't Frank who had invited him anyway. Coming here had clearly been a mistake.

As Kevin got up, Frank reached out and grabbed his hand, squeezing it so hard it hurt. "Kev," he murmured.

"What is it, Frank?" Kevin said, now worried.

Frank tried to say something but kept silent, almost biting his lip as if ashamed. He then let go of Kevin's hand and looked away.

Kevin was not sure what to say. For a moment, his pity for the guy returned. But in the silence that followed, he knew he had to say something. "Maybe I can give you a call, maybe later in the week?" he asked.

"Sure," Frank said, still looking away as if he longed to be somewhere else.

Kevin mumbled an apology that he had to get back to work, then got up and left the garden.

George had been right to call him, Kevin reasoned as he made his way to the car park. Frank was dying. It all made sense now, but what was he supposed to say? He was no doctor. Besides, Frank would only deny it, too proud to admit it even to those closest to him.

It was only as he sat in the car ready to drive off that it suddenly occurred to him why he had made the journey. He hadn't come because he had nothing else to do. He had come because Frank was the only person left alive who had known his mum and dad. He was thirty-nine years old and yet still knew so little about them. For whatever reason, he had never been able to close their chapter or come to terms with their deaths.

They had both died in the first six months of his life, and neither Frank nor Auntie Kay had ever talked about them when he was growing up. He had always secretly harboured the unspoken hope that one day Frank would help keep his parents' legacy alive, but he had never done so. Now, suddenly, this little candle of hope was being blown out.

With Frank dying, the last link to his parents would disappear.

Chapter 5

Frank sat in the medical centre's waiting room, his shirt wet and sticky with sweat. The smell of fresh paint and leather chairs made him feel uncomfortably claustrophobic. His eyes looked longingly at the exit door, wondering if he should make a run for it. Wearing a mask made him feel anxious and, even after nearly a year and a half of lockdown, he had still not gotten used to everybody else wearing masks either. There was something threatening and dehumanising that always made him feel on edge and unable to relax.

The awkwardness he felt today was only accentuated by the unnecessary noise that echoed from the overcrowded room full of strange people muttering quietly into their mobile phones.

Every few seconds it seemed someone's phone vibrated or the ringing tone made him jump up in fear in this open room. Though nobody was looking at him, he felt naked, subconscious about his height, afraid even to look up in case he caught someone's eye and was subjected to scrutiny by some stranger.

Tempting as it was to escape, he knew he had to stay put. He had been having enough problems as it was with nightmares and fainting, but seeing Kevin that morning in the pub had really pushed him over the edge. It had been like seeing a ghost, staring into the eyes of his dead best friend. Perhaps it was because he hadn't seen Kevin for a long time, but coming face to face with him that day was like his spirit had left him and flown back forty years in time and he was once again sitting on the MV *Norland*, looking into Baz's pleading eyes.

"Promise me, Frank."

Kevin was Baz's son. Frank and Baz had been neighbours in Tayport and gone to the same schools. In adulthood, they had remained best friends and served in the army together. Frank had been the one who introduced Baz to his wife, Angie, and been his best man at their wedding, but then their lives had changed drastically when a distant war loomed on the other side of the world and they'd both been sent to the Falkland Islands.

His attempts to forget what he had experienced fighting in that awful war were made harder by the fact that Kevin's father was killed and never made it home, and when Kevin's mum had died not long after the war ended, Frank had adopted Kevin. Despite his good intentions, that had only made the problems worse, especially as Kevin got older. To look at Kevin was like looking at Baz. Every time he saw that kid, the reflection of Baz staring back at him was like looking at his ghost. They could have been identical twins born thirty years apart, both short and stocky, the typical tough rugby type with their obligatory big broken noses. Their wide-boned faces were complemented by their soft and kind blue eyes and childlike black, curly hair. That was why he just clammed up like he had the worst stutter in the world. Butterflies kicked in, and he became overwhelmed with anxiety. Nearly forty years had passed since Baz died and yet to see Kevin was always a reminder of his father and the promise.

Trying to shut out the noise of the waiting room, he closed his eyes.

"Promise me, Frank."

As Frank opened his eyes, he felt a tear forming in his eye. Remembering where he was, he tried to compose himself, afraid the emotion would wash over him.

He turned his focus to the real reason he had come today —his nightmares. It was always the same nightmare, based on something that had happened in the Falklands War. It had been the first land battle, during an ambush at Darwin, a settlement on the way to Goose Green. An Argentinean soldier had been hit by a phosphorous bomb and had burnt to death in front of him. The whole dream seemed to be centred on the rock that had saved his life, hiding him from view of the enemy. The image etched onto his mind, the rock was only about two feet high, barely enough to conceal him. The texture was coarse, a white, greyish stone with an uneven, steeply inclined formation, but it was the unique shape that made it so distinctive and memorable, like two white rocks had been clumsily fused together to resemble a badly formed stalagmite.

What he didn't understand was why it was this incident that played out in his nightmare. There were so many other horrific events he had been cursed to witness, so much about the war he wished he could forget. He had seen ships being sunk with people on board and planes shot down. He had seen things in the trenches that he wouldn't wish on his worst enemy, but for some unknown reason, his brain had deemed that this ambush would form the nightmare he had to endure repeatedly, night after night.

He hadn't had the dream for years, until his mother had died six months ago and it had returned with a vengeance. Now it was more realistic, like he was going to a cinema to see his dreams, not in black and white but colour. The sounds were clearer, the scenery more vivid, the smells more potent. Worst of all, now that his mum had died, his mind had begun tormenting him, pressing on his guilt around her death.

What he had worked out was that the stress and lack of sleep caused by his nightmares had contributed to the fainting episode in the pub, that they had made him paranoid and crazy, causing him to behave so irrationally. As he was browsing a news site on the internet, a simple solution had materialised. Sleeping pills. Of course, why hadn't he thought of it before? They would knock him out and stop the dreams. The prospect of an uninterrupted sleep was the only thing that could save him now. Pills could help him get through the nights, stop the dreams.

So here he was, waiting to see a doctor in the waiting room of Tayport Medical Centre. He had tried to call, but so much time had passed since his last visit that his old doctor had died and he would have to be seen before a prescription could be written. A rare smile had passed Frank's lips as he heard the receptionist speak his new doctor's name on the phone.

"McTaggart."

The name made him smile, memories of old nicknames of his army past rushing back.

He had his doubts, of course. As he casually looked at his watch, he wondered if the pub would be open if he left now. He told himself he would be better in a few months, that the dreams would eventually disappear. However, his thoughts were interrupted as the receptionist told him Dr. McTaggart was ready to see him. Frank reluctantly got up from the chair and followed the receptionist down the corridor, to the office.

The moment the door opened, Frank sighed in disappointment. He had expected his new doctor to be someone his own age, perhaps a middle-aged man with grey hair and a beard. The masked man sitting at the desk looked like the university students George was trying so hard to entice into his pub back in Tayport, a thin person with glasses, dressed casually as if he was soon off for a student party. He was certainly far younger than Kevin. What upset him most was that the doctor did not even bother to stand up and greet his new patient. Instead, he rudely continued talking on his mobile phone, arrogantly pointing at the armchair.

"I'll be with you in a sec," the doctor mumbled, briefly putting his hand over the mobile.

Frank felt the anger boiling inside as the doctor continued talking on the phone. Yet the thought of leaving empty-handed made him stay. He knew he had to be patient. Sleeping pills. That's why he was there. Once he got those, he would be out of there.

Suddenly, the doctor hung up the phone call. "Frank, isn't it?" he asked in a typical Edinburgh accent that made Frank feel uncomfortable.

"Yes," Frank said, intentionally brusque.

"How can I help?"

"I need some sleeping pills."

"Sleeping pills?" the doctor said in a way that made Frank feel he had just uttered an inappropriate swear word. "So, you have problems sleeping?"

"Not really. It's more sort of not wanting to sleep, right?"

"I am not with you. You mean you have insomnia?"

"No, I need sleeping pills for my dreams, to knock me out, right?"

"Knock you out?" the doctor said irritated. "Well, at the very least, Mr. Drysdale, I would need to know more before I write a prescription."

"Why?" complained Frank.

"Because sleeping pills are short-term solutions. Not to mention—"

"Look, Doctor, for God's sake, I am fifty-seven."

"Your age is not the issue here, Mr. Drysdale. Sleeping pills are addictive, and I am simply not allowed to dish them out like sweets. How long have you been having problems with these dreams?"

Frank was getting irritated now. He hadn't expected this to be so difficult. It wasn't like he was asking for heroin. This was going to take longer than expected, and he was ready to leave. He looked longingly at his watch. It was 0905. Opening time at his local pub was less than an hour away. A quick trip on the bus back to Tayport was all it would take. How he wanted to be alone now, sucking in the fresh air, looking out at the views of Tayport. That was the only time he ever felt at ease with life. Talking to some patronising doctor was not why he'd come.

"Please, Doctor, it's really simple," Frank finally gathered the strength to say. "I came here for sleeping pills, so please, if you could just write out a prescription?"

Frank knew instantly from the patronising look on the doctor's smug face that the game was up and he was going home empty-handed. Upset, he wanted to tell him what an idiot he was, that he had served his country and deserved better, but no words came out of his mouth. Not knowing what to do, he walked to the door, opened it, and ran out.

He didn't stop until he had stormed out of the building. Seeing the bus approaching in the distance, he ran to catch it. As he sat down on a bus seat, he tried to calm himself, to catch his breath. As the bus drove off, he felt the masked people in the bus staring at him. Today the bus was full of mothers with younger children. Everything overwhelmed him, the sounds of the bus, the quiet chatter, the mumbling and moaning of little kids. He noticed the driver's face looking concerned in the mirror. The old lady in the opposite corner seemed to stare at him. People pointed. Children whispered. Trying not to draw attention to himself, he stared at the floor, huddled up in his seat and afraid to catch the eye of strangers. He felt like such an idiot now. He had come away without the medication he needed, and it wouldn't be long until sleep came. He would once again be forced to endure that nightmare about his dead mother.

That was the moment he began to hear sounds that drowned out the noises from the bus. Guns started popping nearby, and planes flew low above the bus. He could hear sirens and then noises as people started to panic.

"Take cover, take cover," he heard someone scream.

His heart began to beat too fast, and he shook uncontrollably. And then, as the sound of another jet swooped down towards the bus, he heard the pistol. It was the same sharp, loud pistol shot he had heard in the pub, but this time he knew it was real. He screamed in pain as his right shoulder took the force of the bullet and he fell to the floor. As he lay there, unable to move, he felt the steady river of blood flowing down his back. His chest tightened, and he became short of breath. But it wasn't the pain or the embarrassment of everyone looking at him that he thought about. As his life flashed before him, he felt only shame. This time he really was going to die and the promise he had made his friend Baz would never be kept. He had spent so long putting it off, had wasted so much time delaying it, and now it was too late.

He didn't remember much more. Some of the passengers started to gather around him, asking if he was okay, asking if he needed help, and yelling for the driver to stop the bus. His arms went limp and numb and, as his consciousness began to ebb from him, he tried to mouth the word, "Kevin," but only a whisper came out, quickly drowned out by voices of concerned passengers. The last thing he remembered was hearing a passenger scream. His face turned an ashen white and everything went black.

Chapter 6

It had been a strange day so far for Kevin Turner. His first day back at work and only a few minutes into an important catch-up meeting, the Ninewells hospital in Dundee had called to tell him that Frank had had a heart attack on a bus and was now in hospital. Luckily, the hospital was not far away and, after a quick drive across town, he was now sitting in the hospital waiting room, anxiously waiting for news.

Restless, Kevin picked up a magazine and tried to read, but he could not concentrate. It had only been a week since he met his adoptive father in the pub. Now that Frank was in the hospital, he felt guilty. Was he to blame? Why had he not done more? Now it was too late, the only real reason he was there was so some doctor could tell him Frank had died and was lying on a slab somewhere in the hospital morgue, waiting for a next of kin to identify his body.

"Excuse me, are you Kevin Turner?" he heard someone mumble through their mask.

"Yes?" Kevin said, looking up from his seat.

"I'm Dr. Paul Mayer. You're waiting for news about Frank?" He was smartly dressed, wore glasses, and looked young.

Kevin felt even worse. Probably a junior doctor fobbed off to tell relatives bad news.

"I wondered if we could talk privately?" the doctor asked.

"Sure," Kevin replied. Another bad sign. He assumed doctors were trained not to tell relatives bad news in open places.

After walking a short distance, they arrived at the surgery. Kevin sat next to the doctor's desk, waiting patiently as Dr. Mayer woke his computer.

"You're Frank's next of kin, right? He has no wife or..."

"No, it's just me."

"And you're Frank's son, right?" he asked as he tapped away on his keyboard.

"Well, actually, I'm his adopted son," Kevin said, He looked around, puzzled as he noticed there was no dead body waiting to be identified. "When my parents died, Frank adopted me."

"Okay, yes, I see. I only asked because it appears you have different surnames," he said, shuffling his papers. His face was almost expressionless. "Well, look, Kevin, let me be straight with you."

Kevin nodded, bracing himself for the worst.

"Initially, we believed Frank had suffered a heart attack. Witnesses on the bus said he collapsed onto the floor. To confuse things further, there was a lot of blood from him hitting his head on the seat when he collapsed. Anyway, we have done a few tests on him and concluded that there is actually nothing physically wrong with him."

"Nothing wrong? So, he's alive then?" Kevin said aloud, confused. "But I don't understand. What happened then?"

"He fainted."

Kevin thought he had misheard and froze. "Fainted?" he said slowly. *Wasn't that what George had said happened in the pub garden too?*

"Yes."

"But why?"

"Well, we believe the fainting was caused by extreme emotional stress," the doctor said.

"Emotional stress?" Kevin asked, confused by what the unexpected diagnosis meant.

"Yes," Dr. Mayer continued. "More specifically, it's trauma," he paused as if needing to gather strength to continue. "Kevin, could I ask you something?"

"Okay."

"The ambulance driver said witnesses told him he was holding his arm, moaning he had been shot."

Kevin froze again. He recalled George shouting down the phone at him, "He said someone had shot him, Kevin! Shot him! For Christ's sake, he's losing it mate."

"Do you know anything about that?"

"Well, no, but it's not real."

"That's what we thought too at first, but it soon became obvious that his current trauma is connected to his shot wound."

"Shot wound?" Kevin gasped. "What shot wound?"

The doctor's face looked pained. "Didn't you know that Frank was shot many years ago?"

The word 'shot' felt inappropriate, like someone telling a bad joke at a funeral. For a brief moment, he considered looking around the doctor's desk for the hidden camera. He wondered if perhaps the doctor had been looking for another Kevin or mixed up the patient's medical files.

"Frank hasn't been shot. I don't understand, Doctor. What do you mean?" Kevin said, his voice getting louder with each word.

The doctor said almost in a whisper, "I just assumed you knew." Immediately he tapped away at his computer keyboard before swivelling the screen around and motioning for Kevin to look closer.

Kevin stood up to examine the magnified photo of a small, circular scar about a centimetre in circumference, less than an inch above the right nipple. The scar looked faint and old, resembling a puckered divot. The small area of skin was slightly pinker than normal. Even to Kevin, someone who had no medical knowledge, it looked insignificant, and he wondered why the doctor was showing him. It certainly did not look like a scar someone who had been shot might have.

"And this...this is the exit wound," the doctor continued, clicking his mouse to bring up the next photo.

"My God, Jesus Christ," Kevin gasped, putting his hand to his mouth.

The wound on the back shoulder was much bigger, a couple of inches in circumference. It was messy, jagged, and puffed up like the skin was diseased.

"Are you sure this is Frank?" Kevin asked, still hoping this was all some misunderstanding.

"Yes, of course I am. These were taken about half an hour ago."

Suddenly, Kevin found it hard to breathe. If Frank had been shot, surely he would have known about it? He was his adopted son, had lived with him for eighteen years. There had to be some kind of mistake. Yet he couldn't think of anything that might explain the evidence he was looking at.

"But, Doctor, I don't understand? What's this got to do with fainting?"

"I was just getting to that. You see, these scars appear to be the real reason for his trauma and the fainting."

"How?" asked Kevin.

"First," the doctor continued, oblivious to Kevin's shock, "I should make it clear that I am a heart specialist, but from where I am sitting, it seems pretty clear that his fainting is connected to the trauma of how he obtained the original wound."

"Why? How?"

"Because he cannot acknowledge his old shot wounds. He gets so angry when we mention them or point them out. He looks at us like we are the enemy. It's as if how he got these wounds is so traumatic that he is unable to process them."

"I still...don't...don't understand."

"It's a self-protection mechanism—forgetting the injury ever happened is his way of coping with the trauma. It's a common response to trauma, to represses memories, unconsciously blocking them out due to the stress associated with them. A lot of people with trauma have memory issues relating to the events but rarely so strongly as this. May I ask if Frank was in a war of some kind?"

"Yes, but these scars can't have been from that."

"Why not?"

"Frank was not on the frontline," Kevin said, his voice shaky. "He wasn't involved in the fighting." He was positive that Frank had not been in 2 PARA, the battalion his father had served in. Auntie Kay had told him Frank stayed behind on one of the ships, and for what reason would she have lied about that?

His thoughts were interrupted by further gentle questioning from across the desk. "May I ask what war you are referring to here then?"

"Falklands," Kevin spat out. Even now, decades later, it was a word he hated intensely, the name of the war that had taken his parents away.

"Kevin, I've seen many shot wounds before," the doctor added quietly. "A long time ago, I spent four years as an army medic. I can tell you without hesitation that these scars are easily over thirty years old. You must agree, therefore, that the war you are talking about is the most likely explanation for them. If I were to guess, these would be pistol wounds—9mm, fired from close range."

"Pistol wounds?" Kevin queried. As far as he knew, there were no pistols used in that war. Rifles, machine guns, mortars and grenades were the norm maybe, but not pistols. Besides, the exit wounds he had just seen on the doctor's computer screen looked more like the exit wound of a shotgun. Pistol wounds didn't seem appropriate as the source of this kind of wound. "Doctor, why do you think it was a pistol?"

"Well, exit wounds from pistols aren't usually like this," he continued, "but then the angle it entered is unusual—close range, pointing up. It's all about the trajectory and the close distance it was fired from. This was obviously a serious wound that caused a lot of damage. If I were to guess, the bullet hit his right shoulder bone where it was then deflected."

The doctor waited for Kevin to say something, but he just stared at the computer screen, his mouth open in shock.

"On the plus side, the bullet missed all major organs," the doctor continued, using his index finger to point like he was giving a lecture to his students. "Only minor damage, no vascular injuries, but certainly, the cause of his stiff and painful shoulder."

"Stiff and painful shoulder?" Kevin gasped, staring at the X-ray. He recalled growing up with an adoptive father who often struggled with a stiff right shoulder, unable to lift his arm above shoulder level. Someone who struggled to dress himself and was unable to lift heavy things. When Kevin was older, he had sometimes helped Frank carry things like firewood or coal and believed it was because of a childhood accident.

All the feeble excuses Frank had used made sense now. Not wanting to take off his T-shirt during the summer holidays because he was worried about getting sunburned, not swimming because he claimed he couldn't swim or that the water was too cold.

It had all been a lie, a cover-up, to ensure nobody saw his scars.

Auntie Kay had lied to him too, and all this time he had believed her, taken her word as truth. Why wouldn't he? Auntie Kay was probably the only person in his life who he had ever trusted. Yet now, at nearly forty years old, the truth was becoming clear. This had not been from a childhood accident.

Frank was shot in the Falklands War!

His concentration wavered as he tried to take everything in. For a second, he considered mentioning the fainting and being shot in the pub garden but decided against it. Instead, he nodded politely as the doctor mentioned something about the urgent need for psychiatric help, that he had not seen a more traumatised person before, that Frank needed a good psychiatrist, but he could no longer listen.

It was only when the doctor stood up and thanked him for coming that he realised he needed to get out of here.

Kevin almost ran out of the building as he made his way to the car. Sitting in the front seat, he still struggled to make sense of everything. It was the deceit that bothered him most. Not only from Frank but also from Auntie Kay. The very two people who had brought him up.

Why had they gone through so much effort to lie? War was unpleasant, but to deny you were shot. What was there to gain by keeping such a thing secret? Nothing made any sense.

But, as he got inside his car, another question popped into his mind.

If Frank had gone to such extreme lengths to hide his scars from everyone, what else was he hiding?

Chapter 7

Frank sighed with relief as he poured the cold beer down his throat. Being home after a couple of days in hospital felt so liberating. Usually, he hated this house, but even this hellhole of a place was better than the hospital. The strong medication he had been on the last few days was working well, granting him a temporary reprieve from his nightmares and giving him an inner calm. Being able to sleep and wake up without screaming had been quite a relief, and for the first time in months, he felt like his old self. Even beer tasted good again, Frank thought as he finished the glass. Life was surely going to get better now.

Admittedly, the bus incident still niggled at him. Was it a coincidence that he thought he had been shot in the pub too? This time he had been so sure it wasn't his imagination and that he'd seen blood pouring from the shot wound. It hadn't helped that doctors at the hospital nagged him, saying he needed to talk to a shrink. Bastard doctors, poking and prodding him with their dirty fingers and asking awkward questions about old wounds.

He sighed loudly and walked to the bathroom. The light was off, so he left the door slightly ajar for just enough light to seep through from outside. He took off his shirt and stared at his faint reflection in the bathroom mirror. It had been a long time since he had last seen himself, and he was shocked by his gaunt appearance. Even in the faint light, he could see he was a mess. His face was pale and sweaty, his body too thin. He unbuttoned his shirt and let it drop to the floor. Slowly he lifted his right arm up and put his left middle finger on the scar at the top right of his chest.

Thankfully, time had faded it. It looked so puny, a little bump, partly hidden by his meagre body hair. It was only noticeable because of the little black-brownish spots that surrounded it like a painter had dropped his brush on it by mistake.

"How did you get this bullet wound?" the hospital doctor had asked him.

He wanted to tell him, but how could he when he didn't know? He had no memory of being shot because his mind had blanked out the event. The entire incident had been erased from his memory. He had tried to remember how he got these scars before, of course. Many times, in the very bathroom he was standing in now. Returning home after the war, he had locked himself in here and spent hours staring at his scars in the mirror, racking his brain in frustration as he squeezed and caressed them, hoping for some clue that would help him recall what had happened.

With no memory of the event, all he had to go on was the official version, that sometime near the end of the battle of Wireless Ridge, on the night of the 13th of June 1982, he had been shot by an Argentinean prisoner with a 9mm Browning P-35 pistol. The trouble was that, even all this time later, the official version made no sense. There were no prisoners taken in that battle, and if it was a prisoner, why were there no witnesses?

The worst thing about the whole incident was that he could not remember anything. The only evidence he had was in the mirror in front of him now. The entrance wound scar, the black spots, burning gunpowder residue that followed the bullet out of the muzzle of the gun, indicating he had been shot at close range. There was the clue of the sideward trajectory of the bullet, entering his upper chest from the left-hand side before exiting his right shoulder, implying some kind of close-up scrap had taken place.

Why could he not remember? So many other memories were still fresh as if they had happened yesterday. Ships exploding, and planes being shot down. People being burnt to death or blown to pieces by shrapnel. He had seen things in the trenches that he wouldn't wish on his worst enemy, so forgetting how he had been shot made no sense, and how could a whole battle he had participated in, before, during and after, have been eradicated, wiped clean from his mind?

Perhaps if he had remembered, he would have found it easier to move forward, to accept the truth. But not knowing meant he was constantly thinking about it, going over the possibilities of what might have happened. It was a like a dark cloud, like suffering from dementia and not remembering where you lived.

The irony was that he had spent his whole life trying to forget the war had ever happened. It had happened when he was a teenager, and he refused to let it define him. That was why he'd requested successfully that his military records be removed from public access, as was his legal right. He purposely cut out all contact with his old army comrades. No phone calls were returned, no letters or reunions—everything connected to his past was erased and forgotten.

And yet, it was to no avail because he had no control over his own mind. He had no control over his sleep and nightmares. The curse he lived with was that any reminder of the war was a reminder of his friend, Baz Turner and the promise that still racked him with guilt.

"Promise me, Frank."

It was May 21st, 1982, on the MV *Norland*. The war nobody believed would happen had become a reality. The orders had come through and that evening, Baz was to embark with 2 PARA and go ashore at San Carlos. Frank was to stay onboard and await further instructions. Their cabins were in different sections of the ship, but that evening, Baz had been looking for him. It was an emotional moment because they both knew that Baz might not return. Hundreds of lives had already been lost.

As they'd sat on the bunkbed together, Baz had grabbed Frank's arm. "Frank, if I don't make it back, take care of Angie and Kevin. Tell my boy who I was. Tell him I loved him. Okay, mate?" Baz pleaded, squeezing his arm so hard that it hurt. Kevin was only a few months old, and Baz had still not seen him apart from in photos. As he tightened his grip, Baz looked into his eyes and said the words Frank had never forgotten, the words that had haunted him ever since.

Promise me, Frank.

Even in his bathroom, there was no escape. He could hear Baz begging him as if it was yesterday. That was the last time they had spoken. Baz died in the war and never came home. All these years later, Frank had still not kept the promise. It wasn't because he didn't want to, but because he found it impossible to address the past. The whole war and its aftermath had been so painful that the thought of sitting down and telling anyone, let alone Kevin, about his father was simply too much. The loss of his best friend still hurt to this day. Not a day went by when he didn't miss the guy. Every day he thought about him and the last words he'd said.

Why couldn't he forget the promise. People broke promises all the time, so why shouldn't he? If it hadn't been for Kevin, he would have long forgotten what Baz looked like. And what if Baz had made it home alive, would they still be friends? He had read that they called it survivor's guilt. Apparently, it happened to most people who had been in life-threatening events and lived. Usually, the experience made you feel like an imposter, that they took the wrong person and you didn't deserve to be alive. There was a thought that the guilt had a purpose, to help people find meaning and make sense out of their experiences, that it was a way to express a connection to those who died, a way to keep their memory alive.

Even so, Frank found it hard to agree with that line of thought. No good had ever come from this guilt. Baz had been a good friend, but it was a simple promise made in the heat of the moment. Didn't people make promises all the time in life? How many lies had been told when people got married? I will love you forever? Besides, it wasn't like he had done nothing. He had adopted Kevin when his mum died, hadn't he? He had saved Kevin from the misery of a foster home.

He put his shirt back on and walked back into the lounge. As he sat down on his sofa, he felt sleepy. Frank had been so deep in thought that he barely noticed he was tired. On his new medication, the dreams had stopped so he was no longer afraid of sleep. For the first time in months, there was no need for him to resist his nemesis and he let his shoulders sink into the welcoming softness of his sofa. Unfortunately, the nightmare returned as soon as he closed his eyes—the same dream as before, in glorious colour and cinema sound. The same sequence and surroundings, night-time, cowering behind his rock, afraid to be killed, the deafening noise as his mother whispered to him.

"Why, Frankie? Why?"

As before, there was a big white explosion and a loud scream as the red mist of blood covered him. The fear that engulfed him as he woke up was just as bad as it had been a few days earlier. He felt acute disappointment that his nightmares had returned so soon and yet, as he got ready to run to the bathroom, without thinking, he grabbed his mobile that had been lying on the nearby table and called the first number that came up. Kevin.

"Kev," he gasped, his voice dry and hushed. "Help me…"

REFLECTION

Chapter 8

For the second time in weeks, Frank found himself in a waiting room. Fortunately, this time it was not his busy local doctor's surgery down the road but a quiet private practice in Dundee, the nearest town where he had an appointment to see a Dr. Price, some psychiatrist. Compared to the last waiting room, this one felt more like a luxury hotel, cleaner, whiter, and more spacious. Most important of all, the room was empty, the only sign of life some mother and kid in the corner, quietly distracted by some old paper comic. No people meant no masks to look at.

How the hell had he ended up here, he wondered as he stared out of the window and watched pedestrians scurry around below. It had all started because of the phone call he'd made to Kevin a week ago. Terrified after waking up from a nightmare, he had picked up his mobile and called him. It was Kevin's number that had been on the phone, the last one to call him and therefore the easiest number to reach. After all their strained history, Kevin would have been quite entitled to hang up, but, much to Frank's surprise, the kid had responded well, going out of his way and paying a lot of money to get him an appointment with a Dr. Price.

When Kevin had first suggested a psychiatrist, Frank wanted to object, especially when he discovered that the shrink he had in mind was private, not national health. It wasn't just the astronomical fee that deterred him but that he felt strongly there were others who needed a shrink more. He had heard so many stories about veterans being neglected, about veterans committing suicide. In addition, there were currently a lot of people whose mental health was being challenged by the current pandemic and lockdown. As his problems were not so serious, he felt like he was cheating them, that it was unfair to jump the queue in this manner. Perhaps he was also scared. What if this doctor turned out to be just as incompetent as Dr. McTaggart?

Yet he also knew he had no choice but to accept. Calling Kevin had been the clearest sign so far that his problems were out of control. The nightmares he thought had gone with the hospital medication had not just returned but were getting worse. He knew his nightmares were the root of his problems, to blame for all the fainting and flashbacks. The reappearance of his bad dreams had been a brutal reminder that he could no longer sweep his problems under the carpet.

He looked impatiently at his watch. Two minutes until his appointment would begin. The receptionist called his name and told him Dr. Price was ready to see him. He reluctantly got up from the chair and walked down the corridor.

As Frank followed the receptionist to the office, the door opened and he was immediately taken by surprise. Amidst all the nervous anticipation of today's meeting, he had not considered the possibility that the psychiatrist might be a woman. As Dr. Price walked casually towards him, Frank's jaw opened in surprise. Despite the mask she was wearing, it was not hard to see she was an attractive woman. Indeed, his first impression was that she looked rather like a blonde Nigella Lawson, the celebrity chef he had seen recently on the television. In her early forties, tall and slim with long blonde hair, she had good dress sense too—white trousers and a simple light blue camisole with a soft black leather jacket that highlighted her trim waist and hourglass figure.

"Hello, Frank," she said cheerfully. "I'm Dr. Jane Price. I am so glad you could come today. Please have a seat." She pointed to a black leather chair near the desk by the window.

He couldn't help but smirk. Not only was this doctor a woman but she spoke with a posh English accent, similar to many of the officers he had known in the army.

"You're English?" Frank asked awkwardly, before realising what a silly thing it was to ask.

Luckily, she found the observation more amusing than irritating. "It's that obvious? Believe me, I've spent years trying to get rid of the damn thing. I do hope you won't hold it against me," she said, before gesturing again for Frank to sit down.

"Sorry!" Frank said, shaking his head as he walked over. "I didn't mean to be rude. Actually, I'm English too. I'm from Newcastle originally."

"No problem, Frank," she replied. "So, are you comfortable if we proceed without masks at this point?"

"That would be great," Frank said.

"Good," she replied, taking off her mask and revealing a warm smile that instantly disarmed him.

As Frank finally sat down and made himself comfortable, he had to admit to being slightly overwhelmed. Despite all his reservations in coming here, in just under a minute, this woman had managed to reverse everything he'd imagined a psychiatrist to be. He had anticipated some old, ugly and bald man with thick-rimmed glasses, humourless and stale. Kevin had not mentioned the psychiatrist was a woman when he had dropped him off outside the building. Had he done that on purpose? He made a mental note to strangle him later.

As Dr. Price prepared her folder and looked for some papers, Frank noticed the many paintings and awards covering the walls. She was obviously a successful doctor in her field, having a Doctorate in Clinical Psychology, whatever that meant.

"So, Frank, how can I help?"

"I'm not sure. It's kind of hard to explain," Frank said, wondering what Kevin had told her when he'd booked her.

"Well, give me a clue?"

"I'm not really sure," he said, aware that he wasn't being very helpful, but then the truth was that despite everything that had happened to him, he still didn't understand what his problem was.

Now that the questions had started, he suddenly felt he was in the wrong place. He had never been good at talking about his feelings and here he was, about to attempt to tell a stranger about his problems? And to an attractive woman as well? Suddenly, the cynicism he had felt in the waiting room began to strengthen.

Confused, he glanced at his watch. It was 0905. Opening time at his local pub was less than an hour away. He really wanted to be alone in the beer garden now, sucking in the fresh air, looking out at the views of Tayport. That was the only time he ever felt at ease with life. Talking about problems, that was not him.

"I am having bad dreams," he finally managed to say.

"Okay, and how long have you been having problems with bad dreams?" she asked, smiling as if they were talking about the weather.

"Well, I'm not sure if 'problem' is the right word? I mean, I haven't had them for years."

"Are these dreams always the same?"

"Yeah, the same," Frank said softly.

"Could you tell me a little about them?"

If anybody else had asked that question, he would have walked out right then. His dreams were very personal. Not even his mum, who had witnessed his outbursts for years, knew what his dreams were about. And yet, there was something about this woman. She immediately reminded him of Pat, his ex-wife, with the sympathetic face and understanding smile.

"Well, my dream, it's kind of personal," he told her, buying time to weigh up what words he might use.

"Most dreams are, Frank! That's why it's important to talk about them. I don't need all the details, just the basics. And may I just say, everything you say to me is in confidence. It stays here in this room."

"Right, yeah," Frank said, somewhat relieved she'd told him that. Almost involuntarily, he shifted in his chair. As if to prepare himself, he closed his eyes, hoping it would help him relax a bit and shake off the nerves. "My dream is always the same one," he began. "I was in a b-battle and we were ambushed. I-I was hiding behind this rock...and I-I was..." he stuttered. Even with his eyes shut, he could feel Dr. Price watching him, patiently. He struggled to find more words, but just thinking about the ambush made him shake. This was much harder than even he had expected.

"Frank, never mind. Tell me about your parents," she said effortlessly, changing subjects as if turning the page to a new chapter of a book.

"My parents?" Frank replied, opening his eyes in astonishment at the suggestion. He breathed a huge sigh of relief.

"Yes, you said you were from Newcastle. Were they from there too, and how did you end up in Scotland?" she asked.

"Well, originally my dad was from there. We moved up to Scotland when I was twelve."

"Interesting, and what did they do?"

"Er, my mum was a housewife. My dad was a manager in the shipyards."

"And why the army?" she asked.

"I had this friend...we were neighbours and best mates, but when he left school, he joined the army. It was him who kind of gave me the idea. You know, to join him. At the time, it was a no brainer, as I wanted to piss my dad off."

"Okay," Dr. Price said, smiling.

The atmosphere felt less tense now. With the dreams pushed to one side for the time being, he felt a bit better, but it was her smile that disarmed him most. He couldn't remember the last time someone had smiled at him.

"And what did Dad do when he found out? Did your plan work?" Dr. Price asked.

"Oh, yes!" Frank beamed as he remembered the outrage when he had told his father he was joining the army. His father had wanted him to continue his education, but there was nothing he could do to stop him. Sixteen was the legal age to join the army, and no parents' permission was required. Frank was punishing his father for treating his mother badly, payback for the abusive household he had grown up in.

"That's good," she chuckled.

"I have to admit it that if my friend hadn't come up with the idea, I don't think I would have had the guts to join. At the time, I was young and sort of fooled into believing the army was glamorous, that it would involve travelling all over the world, that I'd meet loads of interesting people." He looked at the doctor and grinned, hoping she would understand what he meant.

Dr. Price laughed. "Yes, I know what you mean. But you know, a lot of veterans I talk to seem to miss those days. Do you miss it?"

"Oh my God, yeah. In the early days, I loved it. I hadn't expected to like it so much."

"Tell me what you miss about it?"

"I don't know. Maybe it was because, for the first time in my life, I felt I belonged. I miss that buddy thing. You know, like being with your mates. You do everything for each other, everyone has your back, so you never feel you are alone. People look after you. It was probably the first time I'd ever felt free, you know, from my family. Of course, I was in a good place too because I was with Baz." Frank suddenly stopped, unable to continue after the enormity of what he had just said.

For years, the word "Baz" had never been uttered aloud before, not even to Kevin, and now he had just said his name to someone he only just met! It felt oddly comforting to finally be able to offload these fears and insecurities to a trusted stranger, and he wondered why that was. Was it because she was a stranger, someone he was talking to in confidence, with no chance of it going outside these four walls? Was it because he trusted her, or was it because, he realised he had spent so long repressing his past that he had also forgotten the good times and talking about them today made him even more aware of just how much he missed them? A reminder of a time long ago when he was interested in life, excited and passionate about things.

"Frank," Dr. Price said almost in a whisper, "you mentioned you were in an ambush? You served in a war of some kind, is that right?"

"Yeah."

"Could you tell me which war it was?"

"The Falklands."

"Oh, I am ashamed to say I don't know much about that war. All I know is that Argentina invaded these islands, a British owned colony. Maggie Thatcher got annoyed and sent off a task force to reclaim them. Something like that. Is that right?"

"Yeah." Frank felt tempted to laugh at the description, but at least she was honest and owning up to her lack of knowledge. He realised that she had a point though. The Falklands War was in danger of becoming a forgotten war, a blip in time, long replaced in the public consciousness by more recent wars like Iraq and Afghanistan. "Yeah, the only problem was that the islands were eight thousand miles away," he added, sarcastically.

"And how old were you when you went to war?"

"Seventeen."

"Seventeen?" she gasped, looking genuinely shocked. "Is that really true?"

"Yeah," Frank said, enjoying the surprised tone in her voice. For a long time, he had been bitter about being sent to war at such a young age. He was just a kid. It never should have happened.

"If I remember correctly," Frank continued, "there were quite a few of us. Back then, you didn't even have to get permission from your mother."

"So, you took a ship over there, right?"

"Yeah."

"Perhaps you could tell me a bit about the journey?"

"Why?"

"Well, I think it might help you to talk about it, and it would also help me sort of understand what you went through."

It didn't take long for Frank to nod his head in agreement. For so long, he had tried to forget the war ever happened, refusing to let it define him. But he had known that coming here today would entail talking about the past, that addressing the past could only be done by recalling it and getting it out in the open. It was more than that, though. There was something special about this woman, and he found it hard not to be impressed by her open demeanour, her presence and the way she radiated sensitivity and concern. He knew that however difficult the subject would be to talk about, there would be no ridicule or embarrassment, that here was a doctor who would empathise and understand.

"Well, I don't know where to start. It was such a long time ago," he eventually said.

"Of course, I understand. Just the basics, of course. I just want to find out what you remember. Anytime that you feel uncomfortable, just say so and we'll stop. No awkward questions, I promise. Is that okay, Frank?"

He nodded and closed his eyes again. For whatever reason, he found it easier to talk when his eyes were closed. As he coughed to clear his throat, he remembered how last night he had watched the movie *Titanic*. He'd been inspired by a scene where the elderly character, Rose, recited her story of how she came to be on the ship's maiden voyage at the age of seventeen. It had struck a chord with him because he had also been seventeen when he was sent to war. "It's been eighty-four years," she had said in the film, "and I can still smell the fresh paint. The china had never been used. The sheets had never been slept in." Recalling it now gave him the inspiration he needed to start telling his story. He leaned back in his chair.

"I was only seventeen when we were deployed to the Falklands," he began hesitantly. "I remember being on a packed train to London on my way back home to Dundee when we got the message to report back to Aldershot for duty. I can still remember the farce of it. I mean, nobody knew where the bloody islands were. I remember thinking the Falklands were on the north coast of Scotland somewhere. It felt like someone was playing a practical joke."

"So how did you find out?"

"I borrowed an atlas from someone and looked it up. That's when I found out the islands were right next to Argentina. Argentina! Jesus Christ! Thousands of miles away. I couldn't believe it. All I knew about that place was something about that woman in a musical called *Evita*. There was also some football stuff, some Tottenham football players were from there, Ardiles, I think one of them was called? Apart from that, Argentina meant nothing to me at all."

He paused to gather his strength.

"Anyway, I eventually ended up on a ship called *Europic*." He opened his eyes and smiled as he said the word.

"What's so amusing, Frank?" Dr. Price said, looking eager to be in on the joke.

"The whole thing was so absurd. I mean, I'd never been on a ship in all my life, and suddenly there I was, on a 4,000-ton car ferry, going off to war!"

"A car ferry?" the doctor almost shouted in disbelief.

"Yeah, you couldn't make it up. The MOD requisitioned a lot of them to get everyone to the islands. It was a very confusing moment."

"Why was it so confusing? What do you mean?"

"I mean, there were huge crowds cheering us off, waving union flags at us. As our ship sailed away, people were parking on the coastal roads in their cars, flashing their lights and beeping their horns. I mean, none of us were marines or anything. The whole thing was like a dream, like we'd won a ticket to Charlie's chocolate factory or something."

"I see."

"But it soon changed."

"How, Frank?"

"I had a bad feeling, especially once we were out at sea. The weather really went downhill. The sea got really rough, and a lot of people got seasick. I kept thinking of my mum and if I ever would come home."

"And when did you realise that war was inevitable? Was there a moment, something that happened?" Dr. Price asked, her tone lowering slightly as if she knew this would not be easy.

"Yeah," Frank mumbled, his mood immediately changed by the question. This was what he called his "9/11 moment," like the twin towers being hit in New York, the rare moments in life when some historic event occurs and you remember exactly where you were and what you were doing. He paused and closed his eyes again, trying to gather up strength.

"I was lying on my bunk bed when my superior officer came in. He said… He said that the *Belgrano*, a big Argentine warship, had been sunk by one of our submarines. Hundreds of people had been killed. That's when it really hit home. That was when I realised there was no turning back, that war was inevitable. I was only seventeen, just a kid, for God's sake!" Frank could hear his voice rising and opened his eyes.

"Do you want to stop…take a break, Frank?" she asked quietly.

"No, I'll be okay," he replied, knowing he had to do this.

"Frank, tell me why you were angry?"

"Until that moment, I never really thought we were going to war. This display of force was all part of letting the Argies know we were coming. Most of us were expecting they would realise their mistake and sit down and negotiate. And now, I felt tricked. I never signed up for war. I just wanted some adventure, to travel a bit, piss my dad off. If I had known we were going to war, I would have never set foot on the ship. I was only seventeen. Too young to go to a pub, to vote, or anything, but it was okay for me to—" He stopped short, feeling almost embarrassed and surprised by the emotion pouring out of him. All the anger of old had come back, the injustice, the deceit.

He took a deep breath before he spoke again, this time, his voice noticeably quieter. "Yeah, hundreds died on that ship, and yet all I could think about was me, me, me."

There was another pause before Dr. Price broke the silence. "You're doing great, Frank," she said, encouragingly.

Frank found it hard to believe he was telling someone all this. For so long, his way of coping with his war experiences had been to wrap them up it in a box, tape it up, and put it away in the corner of the attic where it would never be found. For years, he had erased the war from his memory, ignoring newspapers and opinions, refusing to participate in memorials or reunions. He had cleansed himself of it all and yet it had never really gone away. It had eaten away at him, and now it was pouring out of him like a dam inside him had burst.

"Frank, could you tell me what happened when you got to the islands?"

Frank briefly wondered if it was a good idea to continue. Much as he appreciated her professionalism, it was becoming clear that trying to explain what happened next would be too challenging. Maybe he just wasn't ready to start reminiscing on the terror of being targeted by Skyhawk jets, unable to escape your ship because of freezing sea water, forced to witness the sinking of nearby ships.

"Eventually, I was ordered ashore and then a few days after that, I was ordered to assist the defence platoon," he sighed gratefully.

"Oh, in battle?"

"Sort of," Frank said.

"Was that the battle where you were ambushed?"

"Yes."

"Could you try and tell me a little bit about what happened?"

He knew what she wanted from him, but he felt in a different mood now. Talking about the build up to the war and the journey there had been easy compared to this line of questioning because it was not the war itself. The horrors of real-life combat, the killing and wounding...those were the hardest things to talk about. This ambush had haunted him for years in his nightmares. He felt more vulnerable, more afraid. Suddenly, he felt alone. He knew Dr. Price was behind the desk, that Kevin would be picking him up and driving him to the pub after the appointment had finished, but he was overcome with anxiety. He could feel the anger of those years mounting up inside him, a revulsion that still consumed him. The sheer waste of life. The guilt of leaving all those people behind. He could feel his blood pumping and his hands getting sweaty. He began to retch and tremble violently. Suddenly, he wanted to run again. He longed for escape, to run to the pub and sit out alone in the beer garden. It was Monday, so there would be nobody there.

"Doctor," Frank said. "I can't. I don't want to."

"You've done so well, Frank," said Dr. Price sympathetically. "Let's stop there, okay?"

Frank kept his eyes shut as if he hadn't heard her.

"Frank, are you okay?"

"Yeah. Sure," he mumbled, his body still shaking. He knew the worst had passed and just needed a moment to recover.

"You've been amazing. We can continue with this next time," she replied. "Remembering what you have today has caused you a lot of anxiety, a lot of stress. There are a lot of bad memories coming out of you that you haven't processed for years. It's good for you, but it's also very stressful. We need to take this slowly. You are coming back Monday, and in the meantime, I want you to take these pills, see if they help you." She handed him a prescription.

"What's this?"

"A prescription for Prazosin and Valium. Prazosin helps with high blood pressure, and Valium will help your anxiety."

"Will they help with my nightmares," he almost pleaded.

"Well, there is no medication to help with that long-term, Frank. Only therapy. Have you tried the usual things to try and control them and get better sleep?"

"How do you mean?"

"I mean like not drinking coffee or alcohol, for example. Have some comfort items nearby to bring you quickly back into the present, like nice smelling soap or a glass of cold water. Anyway, we can talk more about that next week. In my experience, the best way to fight nightmares is to talk to people about them. Communication—tell someone your dreams. It doesn't need to be me, could be a close friend or family member. Just get these dreams out into the open."

"Why?"

"By sharing your dreams, you tear them up, ridicule them, laugh at them. By getting them out in the open, you fight back. You take back control! By talking, you desensitise the nightmare, make it harmless."

Frank sat up. "Really? Is that true?" He smiled, encouraged by the suggestion. It seemed a weird concept and yet any suggestion on how to get rid of nightmares had to be worth trying. Whether it was good timing or fate, for the first time, he felt a glimmer of hope. He had now seen a way out. Get the dreams out into the open. Ridicule them, laugh at them. Stop them from lurking in the darkness. He could do that, he had to do that.

"Frank, do you have a friend you can confide in?"

"Not really."

"How about Kevin?"

"Kevin? No, I find it hard just to look at him."

"Well, he obviously cares about you. He's paid a lot of money to get you here."

He smiled at her suggestion. There was a kind of naivety about her. His adopted son, someone he had scarcely seen for years, someone he couldn't look at without wanting to cry. And she wanted him to talk to him about his nightmares? The whole idea seemed ridiculous.

"Well, you need to tell *someone* your dream. I don't know Kevin, but I do know he cares about you. He is close family. You said his dad was your best friend, that you served in the war with him. Tell him these things, get them off your chest. It might help your dreams go away too!"

"I can try."

"Anyway, see you next week then, Frank," she said.

After thanking the doctor and walking out of the room, Frank felt proud. He had managed to survive the whole session without storming out. He felt he was finally on the right track, having found a shrink he could talk to, someone he respected. Someone who held the answers to his recovery. As he exited the building and spotted Kevin in the car, he understood the doctor's suggestion was not as crazy as it first seemed. Whatever problems they'd had before, Kevin was now on his side. The phone call had been the start of a new way forward.

However ridiculous the suggestion of talking to Kevin had sounded just minutes before, it suddenly occurred to him that talking to Kevin was not just about addressing his nightmares but it was also the only way he could ever hope to keep the promise he made to Baz.

Chapter 9

"At long last, Kevin." Frank sighed as he savoured his beer. "At long fucking last. That was hard work, that was. Jesus."

Kevin smiled proudly. They were both now sitting in the corner of the beer garden at Frank's favourite table. Usually, a few hours stuck with Frank in the King's Arms would be an easy proposition to turn down but not today. Frank had made him proud, going to a psychiatrist to face his demons.

It had been a week since he'd received the unexpected call for help from Frank. Initially, Kevin had no idea how to respond. Frank had not called him before, so hearing him pleading for help had been upsetting. He began to feel sorry for him and all the deceit about the bullet wound was quickly forgotten. Perhaps his own separation and the recent lockdown had changed him too. He now felt more empathy for Frank, appreciating why he had chosen to lie about his injuries and was so reluctant to talk about the past. He was quick to remind himself that he had never been in a war and that when people came home from war, they usually wanted to forget, to move on with their lives. Having learnt all he could some years earlier about the war that had cost him his father, Kevin knew better than most that the Falklands War had been a pretty horrific experience. Battles were often fought at close quarters in trenches, using grenades and bayonets. Many had also died in burning, sinking ships hit by enemy aircraft.

Besides, now that Frank had asked for help, progress was finally possible. Remembering what the hospital doctor had said about recommending psychiatric help, he had called a doctor friend who recommended that he book a private appointment with Dr. Price, a top psychologist in trauma. It was expensive, but Kevin had money to spare and his friend had advised that in the current pandemic climate, national health waiting lists were getting longer each day.

Dr. Price seemed to have helped already. The Frank he had just driven to the pub was a very different one from a few weeks earlier. He was more relaxed, unrecognisable from the sick man he had last encountered. Maybe it was thanks to the medication, but he now seemed calmer and more optimistic about the future.

"Kev, thanks for driving me around today," Frank said, disturbing the silence.

Kevin smiled. A "thank you" from Frank was an unusual event even if it was offered without eye contact. "No problem, Frank," he finally said, warmly.

Enjoying the tranquillity of the beer garden, Kevin looked over towards the River Tay. His mind seemed to easily wander out here, watching seagulls searching for food on the deserted beach or counting the swarm of sailing boats as they moved slowly past on the distant shoreline. For years he'd hated this place, but now he finally understood why Frank came here so often.

"That shrink...you knew, didn't you?" Frank suddenly said, interrupting Kevin's thoughts.

"Knew what, Frank?"

"You know, last week, when you booked her? You knew it was a woman, right?"

"Well, yeah, but I didn't think much about that. Why?" he replied.

"She was quite hot, you know. It was a hell of a surprise. I was expecting some old geezer in glasses. She reminded me of that cook woman," Frank said.

"What do you mean?" Kevin chuckled at how Frank's vocabulary could be so discernibly simple at times.

"What's her name? Nigella Lawson!" Frank exclaimed.

"Oh, right." Kevin had heard of her but didn't understand the connection. He had only spoken to Dr. Price on the phone.

"And Jesus Christ, that posh English accent," Frank continued. "She talks like she thinks she's the queen or something, but yeah, she was alright."

"That's good," Kevin said.

"Nice tits too!"

Kevin laughed. Frank had a way of making people laugh when it was desperately needed. It was one of his better qualities, those little moments when you needed a little detour from reality. Sadly, when he got into his beer, it was a quality that disappeared.

"Actually, she reminded me of the ex."

"The ex?"

"You remember Pat?"

There was a name he had forgotten about. He remembered her vaguely from when he was about six years old. To be honest, he didn't remember much, only that Frank had finally gotten married to Pat and they'd moved out of the house. If Kevin was honest, moving out had made his upbringing a little more pleasant. The house was much quieter as a result, and Auntie Kay had become much more relaxed and friendlier.

"My God, it was so weird," Frank said. "I was telling her about the journey to the Falklands and all that. I couldn't believe how much I remembered. I thought I had forgotten most of it, but it was still there. Funny how the mind works. I found it strange to think back to so long ago, thought it would be a patchy memory, but I remembered quite a lot. Little things came back."

"Like what, Frank?" Kevin said, curious. It felt strange to hear Frank mention the war.

"Well, I was telling her about how it all started. The beginning of the war. I almost forgot the send-off we had."

"How do you mean, Frank?"

"The huge crowds that turned up to wave us off at Portsmouth. Bloody thousands of people waving union flags at us. It was a very emotional day. I forgot how proud I felt!"

Kevin stared at Frank in shock. He could never recall Frank mentioning the war in his whole life and here he was, dropping it into the conversation without a second thought. But it wasn't to last. Suddenly, he noticed Frank now staring straight down at the ground, biting his lip as if trying to control himself.

"Frank, you okay?" Kevin could see Frank was troubled by his memories, but his eyes seemed to burn with determination.

"Kev," his voice croaked just like it had last time they met in this pub a few weeks ago.

Kevin felt a shiver up his spine. Was Frank finally going to explain how he got shot?

"Kev," Frank whispered, looking straight into Kevin's eyes. "Ask me something about your dad."

"My dad?"

"Yeah."

"Really? You serious?"

Many times over his life, he had tried to talk to Frank about his father, but it was never the right moment. Frank was always so distant about the war. Kevin felt an inner resentment that he could never tell him. For Frank to talk about his dad, about the war, was taboo, like a dark secret buried deep in the ground. It had caused Kevin a lot of resentment over the years for, however much he understood Frank's unwillingness to embrace the past, the fact was that for Kevin, the past was all he had. The war had changed his life too.

His father had died fighting in the war, but the tragedy was worsened by the fact that his body was never found. He was officially MIA (Missing in Action), a casualty classification assigned to combatants reported missing during wartime. They may have been killed, become prisoners of war, wounded, or deserted but neither their remains nor grave were ever positively identified. It was this one fact that had changed his life. His mother, Angie, had died six months later, after not only having to grieve the loss of her husband but never knowing what had happened to Baz and never having a proper resting place at which to grieve.

All he knew about his dad was what he had been told when he was younger. Frank and Baz had been neighbours in Tayport, become good mates, and joined the army together after leaving home. Both had been sent to war, and Kevin's father had been in 2 PARA, the famous battalion of the Parachute Regiment that fought at Goose Green. Frank had been looking after prisoners of war on one of the ships. When he was a curious teenager, he had tried to find out more but never got far. Reading about the Battle of Goose Green on the internet was always a trial in patience. There was never more than a brief mention of him, if at all. His father had only been a private, so most of the stories about the war didn't mention him. At Goose Green, it was always about Lieutenant Colonel Jones and his Victoria Cross that grabbed the headlines, or the medic who accepted a bottle of vodka as the hundred civilian prisoners got freed. Or how the enemy outnumbered the regiment.

And now suddenly, for the first time ever, he was allowed to ask a question about him. So many years of thinking about this moment, and now that the moment had arrived, the only problem seemed to be what question to ask. Kevin had thousands of them. He felt like a child in a sweet shop with too many choices.

"Well, I don't know. What was Dad like? As a person? I always wondered if he was like me?"

"Your dad...he was the real deal," Frank mumbled. He went on slowly and with pain in his voice. "He was so tough and brave, always waiting for a good scrap, to go to war. So much braver and tougher than me. I remember his determination to go over. Nobody was going to stop him from going. It was like he had waited his whole life for that moment."

As Frank spoke, Kevin couldn't help but notice there was a special wonder in his voice, a kind of idolatry. Even though so many decades had passed, he spoke as though this was the biggest tragedy in his life and it had all happened just yesterday. His hands held the beer glass so tightly as he spoke that Kevin was afraid it would smash.

"But nobody looks forward to war, do they? He must have got scared like everyone else."

"Not your dad. He was a born soldier."

Kevin wanted to ask why anybody would look forward to war, the idea seemed so strange, but he remained silent, afraid to interrupt, afraid to ask too much in case Frank got angry and decided not to continue.

"Kev, you have to remember your dad was only twenty. That's twenty years younger than you are now. He was just a kid. Your dad..."

As Frank fumbled with his words, Kevin sensed something was different. Even with just the two of them alone in the beer garden, the atmosphere was electric, like if Scotland were playing in the rugby world cup final. Moments like this were rare and meant to be savoured. A different Frank was on show today, the tone in his voice more urgent like this was the last chance to tell Kevin what he wanted to say before it was too late. A man getting his books in order, unloading his experiences onto another generation. Today, sitting in this beer garden, Frank had only needed a prod and he was off. Something had opened like a reservoir overflowing. The sadness, the bitterness just gushed out, and Kevin was reluctant to stop it.

Suddenly Frank's smile disappeared. "I can't keep this stuff inside forever. I might not have much time left. You need to know."

"Not much time? What do you mean?" Kevin was worried Frank might get overemotional and become too overwhelmed to talk, but he continued in short bursts, fighting to get his words out whatever the cost.

"A few weeks ago, I was here...in this very seat. I thought, I really thought that was it, that I was dying. I really thought my time was up, and yet all I could think about was that, that I had not kept a promise."

"A promise?" Kevin said, startled.

Frank still looked away. "I made your dad a promise before he died, the last time I saw him."

There was another long silence. Not sure where to look, he noticed Frank's glass was already empty.

"It was after we'd arrived at San Carlos," Frank started again, still with his eyes closed. "We were on the MV *Norland*, and your dad was going to disembark that night. That's when we knew there was no turning back. I remember your dad went quiet. Something was bothering him. Guess he was thinking about you and your mum. He, he dragged me into his cabin...wanted to tell me something. 'Promise me, Frank,' he said to me. I remember he grabbed my arm really tightly. 'If anything happens to me,' he said, 'and I don't make it home...' I tried to stop him, but he just grabbed my arm and squeezed it so tightly that it hurt. He was a strong guy, your dad. 'Promise me,' he repeated. 'Give them a good life, promise me.' " He stopped, as if trying hard to control himself.

"You did give me a good life, Frank," Kevin replied gently.

"It's, you know, I still feel...survivor's guilt, they call it. You know, if only I had done this or that. You know you shouldn't, but you do. It eats you up and all that. But yeah, I've always felt guilty."

"But why? It had nothing to do with you?"

"It's hard to explain. I've always felt like I lived in his shadow, that it should have been me."

"Frank, you adopted me. You did more than was required."

"Anyway, that's why I never spoke about him." Frank sipped his beer. "I'm tired, Kev. I want to go home. Can you take me home?"

"Sure," Kevin said reluctantly. Kevin had been so emotional and involved in the conversation, he hadn't noticed

Frank looked so tired. He still had so many questions, but he could see the whole emotion of the day had finally caught up with Frank. He had been hoping for a little more, but the chat was now over as soon as it had begun. There was always another time.

It didn't take long to walk back to Frank's house. It had been months since he had last been there, and he was shocked by the neglect of the house. Nothing had been washed up or cleaned, old pizza covers lay on the floor. Somehow he felt detached from the mess—now that Auntie Kay was dead, the house had ceased to be the home where he had spent his childhood. Even so, out of respect, he spent twenty minutes clearing up the worst of the mess while Frank had another beer.

By the time Kevin walked back into the sitting room, Frank had already collapsed on the sofa opposite the window. Quietly, Kevin sat down on the nearest armchair and looked at the news on his mobile. Every so often, he looked over at his adoptive father and wondered if he had fallen asleep, but his eyes were still open, staring at the trees outside in the small garden. Only a few hours earlier, he had been full of energy, determined to see the shrink, and now he was almost comatose.

In the silence, Kevin put down his phone, sipped at his beer and watched the television. Soon the only noise in the flat was the voice of the newsreader talking about more bad news related to COVID. He began to hear noises he had never heard before. The pipes creaked, and the wind blew against the open window. Once he assumed Frank was asleep, Kevin got his mobile and prepared to call a taxi and head home.

He was about to make the call when suddenly Frank said, now slurring badly, "Kev...I need to tell...you, please..."

"Okay, Frank, sure," Kevin said. He tried to sound calm, but inside he was very worried about what was coming next.

"I have something important to tell you," Frank said, his eyes now shut and grimacing in pain. He grabbed the nearby remote and turned off the television.

"Okay," said Kevin.

"My nightmare...I want to tell you. Dr. Price told me it was important to...talk about it."

"Okay."

"There was an ambush. We were at a place called Darwin. It was so dark, pitch dark, but the enemy were waiting for us, firing everything they had at us. We were...we were just getting slaughtered. Shit, I was so scared. I was hiding behind this rock." Frank eyes remained shut through a moment of silence. "As I lay there, I thought to myself, *I'm going to die alone on a fucking hill in the middle of nowhere.*"

There was another long pause, then, "But someone...someone threw a phosphorous grenade."

Kevin almost said something, but instinct told him to stay silent and listen. He remembered reading about phosphorous grenades. They could be used as smoke bombs but were also used to clear bunkers. Similar to Napalm used in Vietnam, they reacted with oxygen in the air, burning deep into human tissue.

"Shit, it was...the fucking worst, Kevin. It just burns until...it just never stops until..." After a short pause, Frank gripped the sides of the armchair with his hands and clenched his teeth. "There was this terrible scream up on the hill. It was the enemy on fire from the phosphorous, screaming, trying furiously to put the fire out with his hands, rolling along the grass, trying to extinguish this terrible stuff. Nonstop fucking screaming. It was so loud, so piercing. This guy was covered in fire, like a torch."

He paused, almost unable to go on, his eyes still firmly shut. "I couldn't move for fear of getting shot, so I had to lie there and watch..." Frank now shook uncontrollably.

Kevin sat there in shock, totally confused by what Frank had just told him.

He had been involved in the fighting, ambushed in a land battle at Darwin? But that was part of the Battle of Goose Green, the same battle his father had been in. How could Frank have been there when he wasn't in 2 PARA, the battalion that fought that battle? He'd been certain Frank was not in a battle of any kind. He had been guarding prisoners on a ship.

He was about to object, but as he looked up, he saw Frank was now asleep. He grabbed his mobile and called a taxi. As he put on his coat and got ready to leave, suddenly he gasped. As he stared at the floor next to Frank's body, he noticed a half-empty pack of prescription pills on the floor. These were the pills Frank had bought from the chemist. No wonder he was so out of it. It wasn't the shrink or the promise. Frank had only been talking thanks to a mix of pills and alcohol.

Horrified, he ran out of the house.

Chapter 10

Barely conscious, Frank tried to get up, but the room seemed to swirl around regardless. Those pills were really messing his brain up now. He wished he hadn't taken so many. He had popped in a few pills every time Kevin went to get more beers, hoping they would help him relax. They had done that for a while, but eventually they had made him tired.

He could hear Kevin angrily putting his coat on, calling a taxi, but he was unable to call out to him, unable to stop him. He felt like he was about to faint, but right now, he was so drugged there was no fear.

Besides, he felt a sense of victory at having finally told someone his dream. He had even told Kevin that he made a promise to his father. Dr. Price had told him to tell people his dream, to get it out in the open and disarm it. That's what he had done. He had taken the first step today.

As he heard Kevin slamming the door, he could feel sleep washing over him like a wave crashing onto a beach. There was no anxiety anymore, just a curiosity about what was going to happen. What effect would all the new pills have on the dream? What effect would having told his dream to Kevin have? For the first time in months, he welcomed the sleep.

"Bring it on," he mumbled. "Bring it on."

His nightmare started on cue, but today the dream seemed to start a few minutes earlier as if the projectionist in his head had rewound the spool to the beginning. The noise of combat was the same, but there was no burning body. As he hid behind his rock, he heard his mother's voice further up the hill, calling him. "Frankie, where are you?" It was a shrill voice, the nagging type, like she wanted to grab him by the ear and drag him home. He could hear the disappointment in her voice. He slowly peeked up from behind the rock to look through the smoke. Upon the rocky ridge, he saw his mother, her grey hair blowing up and down in the wind and the faint movement of her dirty white nightdress as it flapped from side to side.

Frank was horrified, unable to comprehend what she was doing on this battlefield so far from home. He wanted to scream at her, tell her she was right in the firing line. He knew it wouldn't be long until the enemy spotted her and blew her to pieces. He had to try and warn her that she was going to get killed if she didn't move.

But he was too late. There was a big flash of light and Frank was forced to put his hand in front of his eyes to protect them from the intensity. The explosion lit up the whole area, and as he peeked up, he could see his mother engulfed in a white phosphorous fire, screaming in pain, trying in vain to put herself out, shaking her arms wildly, rolling herself over the wet grass.

Then it all went silent for a few seconds. The only sound he could hear was the body rolling down, as the momentum carried it downward towards him before it finally came to rest a few yards away to his right.

"Frankie," she moaned in pain as he watched on. Her arms began to flail wildly, as if she were blind and unable to see him.

Frank could hear Dr. Price's voice somewhere, telling him to fight back, not to let his dreams win, but he was too angry.

"Why are you doing this, Mum? You're dead. Leave me alone," he howled.

"Why, Frankie? Why?" his mother's voice whispered.

Before he could answer her, there was a big white flash and a loud scream. What remained of the body exploded, splattering him in a cloud of red mist.

When Frank awoke, he ran to the bathroom to be sick, feeling a glimmer of hope. He felt he had won a small victory in the battle against his nightmares. For the first time, his nightmare had actually changed. It was no longer the enemy on fire but his mother.

Was this because he had told Kevin? Dr. Price had been right after all. The way to beating his nightmares was to talk about them.

As he made his way out of the bathroom and got ready to leave for the pub, a new thought suddenly occurred to him.

Maybe the nightmares weren't really about the ambush at Darwin but about his mother and the guilt of her death. If this was true, the only way forward was to confront his guilt about his mother and come to grips with how she had died.

And accept he had been to blame for her death.

ADJUSTMENT

Chapter 11

"Dr. Price will see you soon, Mr. Drysdale. Would you like a coffee or tea while you wait?" the receptionist asked as Frank sat in the waiting room at the Dundee Medical Centre.

For a second, he was tempted to joke by asking if they served beer, but instead, he politely declined.

It had been two weeks since his last appointment here and he was already feeling disillusioned. A kind of fatigue had set in that made him wonder what the point of coming was. And there had been two weeks of postponements and rescheduling because Dr. Price was too busy to see him. He had wanted to complain. What good was professional advice if you were too busy to give it? However, he had said nothing. It was hard to complain when it was Kevin who was paying for her services.

Admittedly, maybe because she felt guilty about the delays, Dr. Price had called him up on the phone a few times, offering further advice on how to deal with nightmares. She had suggested writing his feelings down on paper or learning what she called "reality checks"—trying to recognise that you are dreaming in the hope that it might help you wake up and thus save you from experiencing the whole dream.

But the more ideas she presented to him, the more disillusioned he became. He could see there had been progress. He was on the right medication. He felt calmer, and the panic attacks of the last few months had lessened in frequency. In addition, the fainting that had occurred in the pub and on the bus had not returned.

Trouble was that while the prescribed medication was working, his nightmares were still there, undaunted by the therapy and medication to quell them, waiting patiently for him to fall asleep before unleashing their fury. Indeed, telling Kevin his dream had changed them but for the worse. His mother had now taken the starring role, and he was forced to watch her burn and fall down the hill towards him.

Dr. Price's suggestion to open up to Kevin had also backfired spectacularly in another way. Hearing all the gory details of his dream had obviously freaked him out as he had not been in touch since. That had been the final straw, making him question what the point of these meetings were. Today would be his last meeting with Dr. Price, he had decided.

"Dr. Price will see you now, Mr. Drysdale," he heard the receptionist say behind him.

"Thank you," Frank said as he got up and began the short walk down the corridor.

Walking into Dr. Price's office, his first reaction was amazement at how different she looked. Unlike last time, she wore glasses, her blonde hair was now tied up in a bun, and rather than the previous colourful clothes, today she was dressed in black trousers and top, ready for a funeral. Last time he had been taken back by her appearance, as if he had been injected with some kind of happy drug. Disappointed, he felt like today was the hangover.

"Hello, Frank," she said, putting on her face mask.

He sat down in his usual chair, facing Dr. Price, ready for another session.

"Sorry for all the delays."

"No worries!"

"So, Frank, how are you?

"Bit better, I suppose."

"Is the medication helping?"

"Yeah, I feel a lot calmer." As he spoke, he wondered if this was the best moment to tell her he wasn't coming back. Should he mention her fee, he wondered. Perhaps when Kevin had stormed out of his house a few weeks ago, he had cancelled the rest of the sessions.

"So, Frank, I've got a lot of stuff I want to discuss today. Last time we were talking about the journey over to the Falkland Islands, so I was wondering if we could continue from there?"

"Okay, I can try," Frank said reluctantly.

"So, this battle where the ambush took place, was it Goose Green?"

"Yeah." *At least she had done her homework,* he thought.

"Can you tell me what you remember after the battle was finished?"

"Dr. Price, I'm sorry but I really don't want to talk about that," Frank said, deciding to be honest. His mind was blank now. He closed his eyes. It had been different last time, talking about the journey over, but now she seemed to want to discuss much harder subjects like phosphorus grenades, exploding ammunition dumps, clearing up all the dead bodies, the terrible smell of war, the icy wind that never seemed to go away. He would keep those memories for himself.

"I understand that, Frank."

"I don't remember anything anyway, to be honest," Frank said, feeling guilty that he was being uncooperative.

"Nothing?"

He shook his head. "Nothing. I only know what I was told."

"Okay, what were you told?"

"Well, what I heard was, about a week later, a lot of us were escorted to Fitzroy by helicopter. Because of the lack of equipment and troops at the time, plans were changed and next thing I knew, I was ordered to help with the final assault."

"The final assault?" Dr. Price looked down and checked her notes.

"Yeah," he said, smiling. Frank liked leaving some bits out. In a strange way, it gave him a little bit of pleasure to see her looking uncomfortable. She had also completely missed the reference to Fitzroy, showing no recognition of the place or its historical significance in the war. "The final assault was the final push towards the capital, Port Stanley, capturing all the main mountains that surrounded it," he said, enjoying correcting her.

"And one of those mountains was Wireless Ridge, was it?"

Frank closed his eyes. It felt strange to hear those two words again. Two words that nobody ever said in conversation or on television, that were even rarely mentioned in the history books. For years he had refused to admit the battle's existence and now some doctor was asking him about it. He nodded reluctantly.

"Can you remember anything about the battle?"

"No," he replied truthfully. He did remember certain events that happened prior to the battle, like when 2 PARA went down with food poisoning from a lamb meal they had eaten at Fitzroy. He remembered vaguely the approach to the mountains in the darkness and remembered the cold weather, but nothing about the battle itself.

"Really? You don't remember anything at all? There must be something?"

"No, nothing. I only know from others that I was definitely there. I took part in the battle, I admit that, but I swear I don't remember anything about it at all. Nothing."

As he spoke, he felt sorry for her. He understood she was only trying to help. She was a professional who had skilfully engaged him to talk about the past, but it had become very obvious these last few weeks that simply talking to someone about past events wasn't going to be enough. Not only did he genuinely not remember so much but even when he did, he found it hard to express his feelings. The first session had been new and exciting. He had been desperate too, at his wits end, but now the events of the last few weeks had taught him that he held the key. Only he could handle the guilt he felt about Baz, his mother, the war. Only he could do something about it.

"Okay, Frank, no more questions!" Dr. Price said, smiling in defeat as she looked at her watch. The atmosphere had changed now. Maybe she had too much to do, too many other patients to think about. She was no longer the talkative, friendly voice of the first session. "I want to discuss the next step for you," she said.

He knew what was coming, some therapy suggestions most likely. "Dr. Price, I appreciate everything you have tried to do, but I've decided that I won't be coming back after this. I'm not interested in therapy and that stuff, so I don't want to continue."

"Oh?" she said, her smile seeming to narrow into a pencil thin line and she twirled her pen around with her fingers, trying to work out what to say next.

"It's been very pleasant talking to you," said Frank, "but I just don't see the point. But I am interested, what do you think is wrong with me?"

"Well, I don't normally give a diagnosis in such a short time."

"I understand that, but please tell me what you think…"

"Well, if you really insist, in your case, I think it's very probable that you have Complex Post-Traumatic Stress Disorder."

The words hung in the air. *Complex? Post-traumatic stress?* He had never thought of himself as traumatised. He was just a guy who suffered from bad dreams. How could it be PTSD when the war had finished nearly forty years ago? Of course, he had suffered for a long time when he came home, but that was decades ago.

"That can't be right," Frank said eventually. "I don't think I have—"

"It is not uncommon for post-traumatic stress to be dormant, to lie quietly under the surface. In extreme cases, like yours, it can take decades to surface," she said.

"But why now?" Frank asked.

"Well, I would guess that something caused it to surface."

"Like what?"

"Well, the current pandemic and the lockdown could have been a trigger. Obviously, I haven't talked enough with you to be completely sure, but I am guessing the recent death of someone close to you could also have been a trigger."

Frank was shocked by the accuracy but remained silent, trying to take in what she was saying.

"Has someone close to you died, Frank?"

"Yeah."

"Well, that sort of major life event can often be the trigger. Would I also be right in assuming your nightmares are about this person in some form?"

"Yeah," he said, looking at the ground. *Wow.* For the first time he understood why she was so good. She had succeeded in getting him to open up and talk in only one session and then almost completely worked him out by halfway through the second session. Frank felt a jolt go up his spine. How did she know so much?

"By the way, that's not all, Frank."

"Huh?"

"Well, you asked for my opinion and I'm afraid there's more. You are not just suffering from complex PTSD but also something called dissociative amnesia."

"What's that?"

"It's when a person blocks out certain information, often associated with a stressful or traumatic event, leaving him or her unable to remember important personal information."

"But why do you think that?"

"Well, you don't remember so much about your war, for example?"

"But...it was a long time ago?"

"Yes, Frank, but there's a lot of stuff we haven't addressed yet because of lack of time."

"Like what?"

Dr. Price lowered her voice and asked, "You were wounded in the war, weren't you?" She softly bit her lower lip.

Frank gasped. Realising he had heard her question correctly, he felt profound shock. How did she know that? Who had told her?

"It appears that how you got shot is so traumatic that your brain has simply blocked it out. What do you think about that?"

Frank remained silent, not sure what to say.

"I was hoping to have a few more sessions with you, but I have to respect your decision. If you are not interested in therapy, then I can't force you, but I do have another idea." Dr. Price seemed to be speaking faster now, as if worried Frank might make a run for it. "It might even be the best treatment for your condition."

"Oh?" Frank asked, expecting Dr. Price to suggest a lobotomy or a month in a straitjacket. He looked at his watch, confirming he'd be out of there soon.

"Sometimes the best way to face a problem is to stare the problem right back in the face. People who are scared of snakes are more likely to cure their phobia by forcing themselves to hold a few snakes and let their brain acclimatise and desensitise. It's the same with a fear of flying or heights. Confronting the reality helps the brain to see that the initial fear is misplaced, exaggerated. Once the fear is out in the open, you can reform it, reshape it, tear it up and throw it in the bin. That's why I told you at the beginning that getting these dreams out into the open is so important."

Frank wondered when she was going to get to the point.

"So, I think you should go back."

"Back? Back where?"

"Back to the Falklands."

"Back to the Falklands? What do you mean? I don't understand." The words Dr. Price had said were completely unexpected.

"I mean you should return to the Falklands, go back there and visit the islands as a tourist. Face your demons. Claim your life back! See them again for yourself. Jog the memory a bit and make your peace with the past."

"Really?" Frank gulped, now feeling sick. The meeting had gone into unexpected territory. Was this some kind of joke? "Are you serious?"

"Very serious! A trip like this would mean closure at the very least. Walk around the islands, watch the penguins and seals, experience nature, absorb the beauty, breathe the air. Visit the cemeteries, pay your respects to those who didn't come home."

"But…" Frank uttered, still in shock from the suggestion. "What about COVID, for a start?"

"You know, Frank, I've been looking into it a bit. With regards to COVID, it's a very safe place. It has a global stamp of approval from the World Travel & Tourism Council as a Safe Travels destination. Right now, October 2021, there is no COVID over there. Sure, you will have to adhere to the strict regulations. By the way, have you had all the jabs?"

"Yes."

"And the booster?"

"Yes."

"Then you will only have to do a five-day quarantine."

"But—"

"Frank, a lot of Falklands veterans have made their peace by going back. Lots of veterans have gone back there. Hundreds of them." She picked up a piece of paper and proudly read out a list. "The Falklands' hero, Simon Weston—I know you've heard about him, the guy from the *Sir Galahad*—has been over there a few times, even met up with First Lieutenant Carlos Cachon, the very Argentine pilot who dropped the bomb on *Sir Galahad* and caused his injuries. Then there was Tony Banks. He took a trumpet he had stolen in Port Stanley back to Argentina and handed it back to the real soldier it belonged to. Nick Taylor, a Royal Marine, handed back a camera film he'd found on Two Sisters to Marcello Llambias, an Argentine he had been fighting against. Graham Ellis returned the ID tag of Argentine Sergeant Ramon Gumersido Acosta, which he'd removed from his body after the soldier was killed. And there are many, many more. Lots of veterans have gone back there. Hundreds of them." She paused to give Frank the chance to say something.

It took a minute for him to say anything. The more he thought about it, the more absurd the suggestion sounded. "But the islands are eight thousand miles away."

"So? They have planes, you know?"

"Yeah, I know that, but you are forgetting something. Even if I wanted to go, there's no way I could afford it. I haven't worked for years."

"Well, that brings me to another thing. The past week, I rang up a few people and made inquiries and found out that it would not be as expensive as you think."

"How come?"

"There are a lot of charities involved who are keen to help, if you agree. The SAMA, the South Atlantic Medal Association, have a Sponsored Veterans Concessionary Flight charge. They told me straight away that you would qualify. Other expenses might be covered by some local veteran charities."

Frank remained silent.

"Look at it from another angle. When was the last time you had a holiday abroad?"

"Don't remember. Maybe it was a trip to Edinburgh a few years back."

"Wow, just think what a trip like this would do for your peace of mind."

Frank didn't know what to say. So much had been said in the last few minutes, and now this idea of travelling back to the islands? The idea seemed too far removed from his reality. The whole world was still locked in a pandemic, and she wanted him to embark on a trip that involved flying thousands of miles, going back to the one place he had been trying to forget his whole life? Just the journey here to Dundee had been stressful enough!

"I really do believe a trip like this might also jog your memory," she continued. "The trip back might be painful, but it's something you have to do if you want to improve. A trip like this will bring you closure. You can't move forward without understanding your past. There is a difference between moving on and moving forward. Once you know the real story, it can lose its power. Eventually, it becomes a chapter of your life and not the whole story."

Frank was too surprised to offer a response.

"Anyway, you don't look convinced Frank, and I get that, but in my professional opinion, this would be the best therapy for you. Much better than drawn out boring therapy sessions, but you have to decide for yourself in the end. This has to be your choice."

"Dr. Price," Frank said, now shaking. She had impressed him not only with her knowledge and experience but also by not offering him the usual traditional therapy. He wanted to say thank you but couldn't. So many emotions were flooding through him. So many surprises had left him unable to talk. There was too much information to decipher.

After a gentle knock, the door opened. The masked receptionist told Dr. Price there was an important phone call.

"Thank you, Sophia," Dr. Price said before turning again to Frank. "I've got to take this call, but, Frank, make peace with your past and the rest will fall into place. Please call me if you want to see me again about anything."

"Dr. Price," Frank said, now shaking. Suddenly he didn't want the session to end. There were questions he needed to ask. There wasn't even time to say goodbye.

However, even before the door closed behind him, he had already dismissed her idea of travelling to the islands. There was no way he was ever going back there. They were the islands of hell that had cursed his life. He would rather die than return.

His thoughts turned to the realisation that this would be the last time he would see Dr. Price. Even if she were just a pretty psychiatrist, she had brightened up his day far more than the boring scenery in his beer garden. She was a hundred times more interesting than the old haggard faces of the pub regulars with their lifeless and defeated eyes. She had shaken him up, a reminder of just how empty his life really was. She had made him reflect on his boring life, temporarily brightened it up and brushed away the dust.

That was really what bothered him. Loneliness. For a little while, he had found someone to talk to, to challenge him, and now, thanks to his decision not to come back, he was back where he'd started. Alone, with nowhere to go but the local pub. With Kevin no longer talking to him, there was not much to look forward to anymore.

Chapter 12

Even as Kevin sat in the beer garden of the King's Arms, he still couldn't believe he had agreed to meet up with his adoptive father again. Only a few weeks earlier, he had naively offered to help Frank, paying for a private psychiatrist, picking him up and driving him to the pub. The whole day had been a farce. It wasn't just the sight of all those empty pill packets that had upset him, it was the lies. Spaced out on pills and alcohol, Frank had glibly claimed he'd fought alongside his dad at the Battle of Goose Green and that he had also been with his dad on the MV *Norland*, the ship that had been used to transport 2 PARA over to the islands.

There was simply no way Frank had ever been in 2 PARA. Paratroopers were mentally and physically tough, elite soldiers, highly experienced and well trained. He found the idea of a tall, lanky, clumsy Frank filling those shoes so unlikely, so impossible. Just to be sure, he had even checked the paratrooper database websites on the internet. As he had suspected, Frank Drysdale's name was not on any of the lists.

For a while, Kevin had considered the possibility that Frank was a Walt, a military imposter making false claims about his military service, but over the last week, he had softened his attitude. He deserved the benefit of the doubt.

Perhaps there was a simple explanation he had not considered for the connection with 2 PARA and his father. Moreover, an article he had read a few days ago about Falklands War veterans further changed his perspective.

The article had been about how most veterans never talked about their war because they felt their story would be "too much" for others to hear, that the listener wouldn't be able to manage the very raw details or surge of rage or the tears that follow close behind. Most felt they could never capture what really happened over there, so didn't bother. The fact that Frank had tried hard to open up made Kevin wonder if perhaps he had been making the wrong assumptions about him, that maybe he had misinterpreted what had been said. Perhaps the truth behind Frank's story was so traumatic that his mind needed time to work it out.

Now that Frank had finally begun to address his war issues, Kevin should have been encouraging him, not doubting everything he said. Indeed, just browsing the war on the internet over the last couple of weeks had been enough to make him understand Frank's inability to talk about the past. The systematic failure to prepare veterans for the horrors of war and to provide adequate care for them afterwards was deplorable. A huge majority of veterans had been left emotionally scarred and unable to work, immersed in social dislocation, alcoholism, and depression. These veterans had suffered prolonged personality disorders, flashbacks, and anxiety resulting in hundreds of suicides that continued to the present day.

Suddenly, he felt guilty for being so impatient with Frank. He had been so keen to learn more about his father that he had ignored the real issues troubling Frank. That was why, on hearing Frank apologising yesterday on the phone and begging for another chance, he had mellowed and agreed to meet him.

Of course, guilt wasn't the only reason he had changed his mind. All the recent talk with Frank had also reawakened his interest in his parents. He had spent so long trying to forget his parents had existed that it was only now he had come to realise he was actually still grieving for them.

Times had changed dramatically since he'd last shown an interest in his parents' past. Back then, when he was around thirteen years old, the internet was still in its infancy. Communication was via email only, and internet connections were charged by the minute. There was so much more material to look at now, like videos on YouTube, hundreds of online autobiographical books written by veterans, and Facebook. All he needed was the courage to contact the veterans themselves.

"Hi, Kev!"

Kevin looked up. Frank was walking towards the table, holding two pints of beer. Frank had never bought drinks for him before, yet he was more taken aback by the improvement in Frank's appearance. He looked so different from the last time—more himself and not so tired, calmer and less anxious. For a second, he thought it was someone other than Frank, so remarkable was the transformation.

"Thanks, Frank," Kevin said, taking one of the beer glasses. "How are you?"

"Yeah, good." Frank sat down and took a large gulp of beer. "By the way, thanks for coming today."

"No problem."

"No, I mean it, mate. Like I said on the phone, I know I fucked up last time. I know I took too many pills and said some stupid stuff."

Kevin knew this was the right moment to be upfront. There could no more lies this time. Frank had told him too many half-truths last time, and after years of not telling him anything at all. If this relationship was going to work, Frank needed to be honest and forthcoming.

He looked his adoptive father in the eyes and said, "Frank, if you really are sorry, I think you need to be more honest with me."

"How do you mean?" Frank said, seemingly hurt by the accusation.

"Like, when you mentioned that you were at Goose Green?"

"I was at Goose Green, Kev, and so?"

"You were? But you weren't in 2 PARA?"

"No?"

"You were on the ships?"

"I was to start with, yes."

"But then how did you end up in the battle?" Kevin asked.

Frank took a deep breath and then looked away, as if gathering the necessary energy to explain. "I was still training when the war broke out, so I never did P Company."

"P Company?"

"Yeah, google it sometime. P Company is the main test you need to pass to become a PARA!"

"Oh, okay."

"When it became clear that we were going to war, nobody knew what to do with me. I was training as a medic, so the forces thought I might be useful in helping the wounded and decided to bring me along."

"Oh, right," Kevin said, embarrassed. Still, the thought of Frank being a medic seemed odd.

"I know what you're thinking, Kev. Me being a medic? All I can say is that it was a very broad definition back then. The very basics of medicine was what it was. Anyway, eventually they decided to put me on a ship called *Europic*."

"*Europic*? But you said you spoke to my dad on the MV *Norland*?"

"Yes, but that was when we got to the islands, Kev. I was transferred to MV *Norland*, 'cross decked' they call it, and that's when I saw your father."

Kevin nodded, feeling like a child being scolded or a teacher telling him off for not doing his homework. He should have done a bit more research rather than simply assume Frank was lying. "Sorry, Frank."

"It's okay. Your dad disembarked and headed off up the mountains with the rest of 2 PARA, but I stayed in San Carlos."

"So how come you fought in the same battle as my dad if you stayed at San Carlos?"

"Okay. I'll try the short version. I stayed on the ship, waiting for orders. Originally, I was assigned to look after any prisoners of war, but after a day or so, I was sent ashore to help at San Carlos. Actually, to be honest, I was so desperate to get off the ship, I begged my superior officer to let me go ashore."

"Why?"

"Bomb Alley."

"Oh, right," said Kevin. He knew the basic history of the war. Bomb Alley was another name for the group of battles that took place at San Carlos, where the British had landed. Low flying Argentine jets had repeatedly attacked the British ships over a few days with surface to air missiles, causing severe human losses and damage.

"Anyway, after helping out at San Carlos and Ajax Bay, I was assigned to assist the defence platoon."

"But why did they need you then?"

"Very simple, Kev. Trench Foot."

Kevin nodded. "I read about that. One of the ships that had been sunk was the *Atlantic Conveyor*, which carried a lot of the helicopters that were going to be used to transport everyone around the islands. The sinking meant most people were forced to walk everywhere. The problem was the terrain and weather conditions were so bad. Everyone had to walk for miles and miles with heavy equipment on their backs and the ground was so damp and soggy. Their army boots were not designed for these conditions and got waterlogged."

Frank turned to look at him and smiled. "Yeah, that's right. Well done. The foot becomes numb, changes colour, swells and starts to smell due to damage to the skin, blood vessels and nerves in the feet. It can take three to six months to fully recover. Anyway, basically lots of people went down with it and they ran out of fit folks, right? The terrain wasn't ideal either. There were a lot of broken ankles and stuff."

"Okay."

"Anyway, basically they ran out of people. That's how I ended up in the battle. I was ordered forward to assist the defence platoon with clearing bunkers and resupplying ammo."

Frank drank a few more sips of his beer and gazed out to the River Tay. It was a welcoming chance for Kevin to digest everything he had told him. Everything made more sense now.

So, Frank had been in a battle after all, with 2 PARA? Auntie Kay must have lied about that too, or maybe she had never really known what happened because Frank had never told her?

"Kev, how much do you know about the battle?" Frank said, now looking at Kevin.

"You mean Goose Green?"

"Yeah."

"A bit," Kevin replied. He'd tried to learn more about the battle on YouTube, but as there was no real footage of the battle, it was hard to imagine what it was like. All he knew was the official version because during the war, there had been strict government control on any outside media coverage, which had frustrated his earlier efforts to discover the truth.

"Okay, tell me then. Remind me," he said painfully as if trying to be brave.

"Well, Goose Green was the first major land battle. The objective was to make a five-mile trek to Goose Green and take out the main enemy defence located on Darwin Hill along the way with the help of artillery support. After sixteen hours of fighting, the enemy surrendered. But there was a cost." Kevin thought about how history was different when it had a direct effect on you personally. "Eighteen dead and sixty-four wounded."

"Yeah. That sounds right. The reality was rather different though."

"How do you mean?"

"Well, it was dark for a start. And then there was the noise," he said dejectedly.

It looked like certain memories were starting to come back. He looked like he was fighting to remain in control.

He made a grimace, like he had swallowed a bad oyster. Kevin wondered what he was thinking about. He could feel the anger mounting up inside him from across the table and wanted to say stop, but he didn't dare.

"You know, what really pissed me off was that the general public was never told what was really going on," Frank said, his voice getting louder and angrier with each word. "It was always the official version that people heard, how the heroic Lieutenant Colonel Jones," he now spoke in a sarcastic, whining tone and looked up, "his unit pinned down by heavy fire, bravely stormed the entrenched enemy positions despite being completely outnumbered by the enemy."

Kevin had never seen him so angry. His eyes looked tired and confused.

"The British public love a good fucking story, don't they? Who cares if it's true or not. I'll tell you the truth, Kevin. The battle was a load of cock-ups from start to finish," he said, spitting the words out. This was quickly followed by a long silence as Frank tried to calm himself down.

"Sorry, Frank."

"For what?"

"I don't know, bringing it up. It must have been terrible," Kevin said.

"Yeah well, it was a long time ago. It's about time I addressed it," Frank said. "Besides, I think it's only fair that you know, understand what your dad was up to and stuff."

Kevin didn't want to ask the next question. He was afraid of pushing his luck, but he also knew there would never be another chance like this. "Frank, last week you said the last time you saw my dad was on the ship."

"Correct."

"So that means you didn't see my dad in the battle," Kevin said tentatively.

"Yes, that's right. You have to remember, there were hundreds of people in 2 PARA, plus all the Royal Marines. We all had different objectives. I never saw your dad. He was frontline. I was support. I was clearing bunkers and helping take care of any prisoners we encountered."

"Frank, they said eighteen British died in that battle," Kevin stuttered now, nervous about the subject matter. "But those numbers don't include my dad, do they?" he asked even though he already knew the answer.

"No, Kev. They don't." Frank sighed loudly and clasped his hands together, preparing himself for what he was about to say. "Like I said, I never saw your dad. All I remember is that at the end, I was helping to supervise prisoners when someone told me your dad had suffered grenade shrapnel injuries. It was not serious but bad enough that it needed urgent medical attention."

"So, Dad was evacuated, right?"

"Yeah, the worst injuries were sent to the hospital boat called SS *Uganda*. But lesser injured people, most people like your dad, were taken to Ajax Bay."

Kevin nodded. He had read about the field hospital at Ajax Bay, near San Carlos, where the Allied forces had landed about a week before. Back then, it was nicknamed "The Red and Green Life Machine." It was an old refrigeration plant situated next to an ammunition dump. At the time, it was the only place available in the area that had adequate roof cover. He read that the conditions in the field hospital were basic and poor. Despite this, of the five hundred and eighty British wounded soldiers and marines treated at the hospital, all of them survived. It was this statistic that lay at the very heart of the dilemma of his father's disappearance. If his father had gone to Ajax Bay, he must have survived, especially as shrapnel injuries were not usually fatal.

So why had he never come home? Kevin asked quietly, "So, what do you think happened Frank?" The six-million-dollar question had now been asked.

Frank sighed. "I wish I knew. It took me years to accept that he wasn't coming home. I always hoped there had been some mix-up. I always hoped that one day your dad would just walk through the door, that it had all been a mistake. I never saw him die. I never got the chance to say goodbye or anything. There was never a proper funeral because they never found his body."

"But why not?" Kevin asked bravely, now entering un-charted territory. All his life, he had been waiting for the right moment to ask Frank about his father and now it was finally happening.

"I don't know, Kev," he replied reluctantly. It was the Frank of old for a second.

Kevin had come so far now and had to keep asking, to take advantage of the promise that Frank had made. "Please, Frank, tell me what you think. Could it have been friendly fire?"

"Doubt it. There were some incidents in that war, but even if it had been friendly fire, there would have been a body."

A body, thought Kevin. It had taken him years to under-stand the fact that no body ever being found was the real reason his mum had died. The Missing in Action label had pushed her over the edge. She had no body to bury, no resting place, no great comfort from the usual traditions and ceremonies normally associated with death and dying.

No closure and no healing. No funeral. It wasn't cancer that had killed her, it was a broken heart. All those months of waiting. She must have struggled with not knowing whether he died peacefully or had a horrible death.

"I think it was a cover-up," Frank whispered as if he was worried someone might be spying on them.

"A cover-up? By whom?"

"The Thatcher government."

"What? But why?" Kevin replied.

"Well, think about it. By all accounts, your dad was sent to Ajax Bay. But then, about a week later, nobody is quite sure when or why, he just disappeared. His body was never found. Many theories were put forward, like maybe he was captured and killed by the enemy after being discharged. Or that he got injured as he made his way back to his battalion. Some claimed he had defected to the Argies. Some said he had some kind of breakdown and hid on one of the many islands nearby. That he deserted, lost his nerve."

"You don't sound convinced when you say that, Frank."

"Of course not. It's complete bollocks. I knew the guy. He was the toughest, most loyal, bravest man I ever met. That war was his mission in life, his dream. There was no way he would desert. These theories are crap. That's why I think it was more likely a cover-up. The Thatcher government covered it up."

"But why would they do that, Frank? What would be the point? What would they need to hide? He was just an ordinary soldier!"

"Well, no official explanation was ever given. It was as if we were expected to just forget it. I sensed something fishy was going on, always have. I sometimes wonder if it had something to do with the SAS?"

"SAS? What do you mean?" All he knew about the SAS was that it was the special forces unit of the British army. They specialised in undercover activities, mostly classified, due to the sensitivity of their operations.

"Well, they never found his body, Kev. His dog tags were never found. And then, about a week or two after we had returned home, when people started to get angry about the lack of information, the Ministry of Defence suddenly decided to refuse to answer any more questions on the subject, issuing a statement that he was presumed killed, missing in action. All of us who were there knew that was a blatant lie. We had many first-hand witnesses who had seen him very much alive. There were some of 2 PARA and others at Ajax Bay who remembered seeing him. The timing was dodgy too. They cynically waited until most of us had gone home before they told everyone the lie about him getting killed. They obviously wanted to avoid the media getting hold of it."

"But, Frank, my dad wasn't trained for the SAS."

"True, but we don't really know that for certain. There are things we now know about the SAS that we didn't know back then."

"Like what?"

"Secret missions to get rid of the Exocet missiles and stuff. Wasn't there some trip to Cuba or something? Maybe someone messed up and there was one big cock-up. Think about it. I wasn't really qualified to be in the Battle of Goose Green, but I was still used. They say you do the job with the army you have. With all those people going down with trench foot, the wounded, they had to adjust. The SAS lost a lot of men, and helicopters were lost. They needed more resources, and your dad was good material. Maybe the fact that he was not in the SAS was actually the reason they used him? It would mean fewer people would suspect anything. There was a lot of covering up going on, Kev. Everybody was very keen to brush things under the carpet after the conflict. We had just won a war and nothing was going to spoil that. That's why it was never explained."

Kevin had never thought of this, but right now, despite coming across as far-fetched, his curiosity had been aroused. Already he doubted there was anything to it. Even if his dad was a secret SAS operative, why cover it up? However, he made a mental note to look it all up when he got home. Looking at Frank, he said, "Thank you for being so open with me. I'm sorry that I didn't believe everything you said before."

"Kev, the war was really nasty. That's why I never talked about it. Some of my mates were in bits. I saw men with no heads. Guys with no legs, no arms. That sticks, and you can't get it out of your mind. You come home and no one does anything about it. I'm just saying."

"Why now, Frank?"

"Because I'm tired and because of your dad. I promised him, right?"

Thinking it was a good time to change the subject, Kevin said, "By the way, how are the meetings with Dr. Price going?"

"Nah, I've decided to jack it in."

"Oh? Any reason?"

"It wasn't for me. All this therapy stuff. I think it's enough that I'm telling you everything."

Kevin understood what Frank meant. Frank had always been the impatient type, unwilling to show his feelings, but today's conversation made him realise that Dr. Price's sessions had achieved something. The change in Frank addressing the past had been quite extraordinary. Or was it all simply down to a man struggling to tackle his demons? Or was it the guilt of the promise he had not kept?

"Kev, you know." Frank smiled. "This shrink? She had this crazy idea…"

"Oh, what was that?"

"Well, she said,"—Frank chuckled as he spoke—"as I wasn't interested in therapy and all that, I should consider going back."

"Going back? Go back where?"

"Go back and visit the islands." Frank almost scoffed the words.

"Oh?"

"Yeah, that's what I thought. Confront the past, she told me!"

"Confront the past?"

"Yeah, you know."

"Well, *is* it such a bad idea?" Kevin asked more out of politeness than anything else. It did seem a strange idea, especially as there was still a global pandemic going on, not to mention the fact that Frank hadn't travelled for many years.

"Kev, it's a terrible idea," Frank said, offended. "It's not for me. I don't think I could handle it. Even without COVID, I would struggle. Going all that way on my own? I mean, to start with, it's a twenty-hour flight or something."

"Right," said Kevin, now regretting he had queried the idea.

"Of course, she doesn't seem to understand one very important thing."

"Oh, what's that?" Kevin asked, expecting Frank to say something like it had taken him almost forty years to even talk about the war, let alone revisit the battlefields themselves.

"She forgets I have no money. Maybe she thinks I am paying for her sessions and not you. A trip like that would cost thousands of pounds, which I don't have." Frank stopped. All of a sudden after three beers, he looked very tired. The whole emotion of the day seemed to catch up with him all at once. "Kev, I'm going home. Do you want to come back for a beer?"

"No, I've got a meeting at work," Kevin lied. Frank wasn't drugged or drunk this time, but Kevin wasn't ready to take the chance that he would remain so. Besides, he had a lot of new information to investigate and it was best to leave on a good note. "I'll call you later, okay?" Kevin said, getting up and making his way to the car park.

As soon as Kevin got in his car, he felt dizzy and took a deep breath. For the first time in his life, he understood what shock did to the body. He sat there unable to move, unable to focus. Frank had opened up about so much of the past, and it was all so overwhelming. He wished he had recorded it all or written it down on his phone. He went over in his mind what they had discussed, afraid he would forget something. He had learnt so many new things about the war and the theories about why his father never came home. However, as he got ready to drive, one of the last things Frank had said refused to go away.

"Confront the past," were the words that Dr. Price had told Frank. The idea of travelling back to the islands and making peace with the past. He suddenly realised he was no different from Frank. He had spent his whole life hiding

from the past, trying to forget he ever had parents, refusing to let their deaths define his life. He had spent so long criticising the guy for not being the perfect father figure, for not telling the truth, yet he was no better! He was guilty of the same crime. Now Frank was trying to confront his past, and it was time for him to do the same too. He knew what he had to do. He owed it to his mother and father to find the truth of what happened to them. He owed it to Frank and Auntie Kay too.

"Of course!" he shouted out loud, banging his hands on the steering wheel.

Excited, he picked up his mobile and dialled Dr. Price's number.

Chapter 13

There wasn't much of a view outside Frank's house. Overgrown trees hid much of the garden, but it was the fresh air coming in from the open window that helped him focus, helped him get his mind off the more unpleasant stuff. With the window open, he could hear the world continuing, the heavy rush of cars and birds singing.

It also helped him forget the emptiness of the house. Since his mother died, he had missed the sounds of her presence. The usual small talk about weather, the muffled footsteps as she limped around the house, the clattering of china teacups in the kitchen. This was the house he had lived in most of his life, but it was also the house his mother had died in. Every day he was here was a reminder about how lockdown had strained their relationship to the point of no return. Just like his war, his way of coping was to block it out—it was easier that way. To be in denial, that's how he coped.

Restless, he walked back to his sofa and sat down. It had been almost a week since the phone call from Kevin. He had been very excited about this great idea based on Dr. Price's suggestion that Frank go back to the islands and sort out his issues. The difference was that Kevin would be coming with him and paying for the entire trip. Frank wasn't sure exactly what costs were involved in this grandiose idea. He guessed it would be thousands of pounds, but when he had objected, Kevin had been unfazed, claiming he had worked hard for years and could afford it.

Kevin was not just paying for all the flights but also the cost of staying in a hotel throughout the trip. Covid would not be a big problem, but as they had both had all three jabs and a booster, they would have to do a five-day quarantine in the hotel upon arriving.

Kevin had even been in touch with Dr. Price, who had agreed to ensure Frank had enough medicine for the journey. In fact, the only problem was the timing. Kevin was insistent that the best time to go was in November when the summer season started and the weather was more agreeable and, because he was unwilling to wait another year, that meant going next month.

Frank found it difficult to object. The kid seemed so excited, convinced this was a brilliant move.

"All you need to do is say yes and I will do the rest," Kevin had said. "It will cost me a bit, but I don't care. It will help me too, knowing that I helped you in a small way, and I can also make peace with my dad. I can afford it, so don't worry!"

Luckily, Kevin had given him a week to think about it. If Frank agreed to come, they would leave in four weeks.

It had been a hard week for Frank, trying to come up with a decision. He found it hard not to be negative about it, not to think the worst. He found the prospect of flying halfway across the world daunting, terrifying. The estimated flight time was at least twenty hours, and that didn't include all the stopovers at other airports. It was a long journey for someone who had never flown before.

He also worried about the effect the trip would have on his nightmares. Even after all he had been through in talking about this history for the first time, he was still suffering from them. What would returning to his islands of hell do to his frail mind? Would going back simply dig up much scarier memories? Was it really possible, as Dr. Price had tried to convince him, to make peace with one's past? What if she was wrong? What if this trip only made everything worse?

But today, after another sleepless night, he had made his mind up to go. How could he not go? Wouldn't going back address his survivor's guilt? Wouldn't going back mean keeping his promise? Helping Kevin understand who his father was, to visit the very place where he had died, to let the lad walk in his footsteps and even possibly try and solve the mystery of where he had lost his life was not something he could deny. This trip was also a golden opportunity to pay his respects not only to Baz but to all the soldiers who had died over in the Falklands serving their country.

There was another reason he had to go. He walked over to a drawer and took out a framed photo. His mother had loved this photo, though he hated the reminders of the past. It was an old photo taken with an instant Polaroid camera from the 1970s of a young couple on their wedding day, and the colours had faded with age. Kevin's mum and dad were holding the cake knife, about to cut into the wedding cake and make a wish. As they did, they gazed adoringly at each other, as if the other guests didn't exist. Angie looked radiant in her white wedding dress, and Baz looked dapper in his black dinner jacket and tie, the proudest man in the world. To their right, poking his head into the photo, was himself, the best man.

Seeing this photo always made him sad. He looked almost unrecognisable—happy, youthful, smiling as he made an awkward funny face to the camera, oblivious to what lay ahead in the future. This was the Frank his mum missed, the forgotten Frank. The Frank he had abandoned. Not long after this photo had been taken, a war had broken out and he and Baz had been sent across the world. The war had changed him forever. Was that why his mother had liked this photo so much? Was it a reminder of what she had lost?

She'd always told him that he came home a different person, and he knew what she meant. Those early years had been a blur of alcohol, depression, and bad tempers.

That's why he had to go back. Whatever challenges he would face, he owed it to her to find the young Frank, the Frank that had been lost.

It was her death that had started everything too. He remembered Dr. Price mentioning that her death had been a trigger, what caused his nightmares to resurface and his post-traumatic stress to fully show itself. Maybe going back would help his nightmares. Dr. Price had certainly been right about one thing. Telling Kevin his dream a few weeks ago had changed the dream from a dead body whispering to him, to his mother walking around on the battlefield.

Maybe opening up to Kevin a little more about her death would have an effect on his guilt and nightmares.

Why, Frankie? Why?

Yes. Maybe it was time to tell him the truth about Auntie Kay. He picked up his phone and called Kevin.

Chapter 14

Kevin was in a good mood as he drove to Frank's house to discuss the travel itinerary. Today was the start of his month-long sabbatical from work. The trip had now been booked and fully paid for. Admittedly, it had been difficult persuading Frank to come, but the other day he had finally agreed and, in a few days, they would be flying to the Falkland Islands.

The more he thought about it, the more it seemed the trip of a lifetime—a golden opportunity to retrace his father's footsteps—and tolerating Frank for a few weeks seemed a price worth paying. It would have been preferable to have a few more months to prepare, but November was summer in that part of the world and the only feasible time to go. Not only could he not bear waiting another year, but also, because of COVID restrictions, the islands would be quiet and more agreeable for Frank as opposed to the crowded 40th anniversary celebrations expected next year.

However, he had to profess the costs involved were mind boggling. The cheap concessionary flights Dr. Price had mentioned flew from Brize Norton near Oxford, and getting there from Scotland made the full price charter flights from Glasgow to the islands via Chile and Heathrow the better option. The hotel wasn't cheap either, but the thought of sharing a room with Frank had made him cough up for two single rooms. Another huge cost had been comprehensive travel and medical insurance, even higher than usual due to Frank's age and the still lingering pandemic. Fortunately, Dr. Price had agreed to prepare Frank with enough medication for the trip. Frank now had pills to help him sleep, pills for his nerves, and even pills for possible air sickness.

Now that the trip was going to happen, Kevin had discovered a new lease on life. No longer distracted by his marriage problems or his career, instead he had spent his energy the last few days on researching the war, in preparation, determined to find answers to the questions that had affected his life. It was only now that he appreciated how the Missing in Action label had pushed his mum over the edge. The emotional toll the unknown had had on her, the years of anguish and dealing with all the emptiness. It wasn't cancer that had killed her, it was a broken heart. All those months of waiting. She must have struggled with not knowing what was his dad doing when he died? Did he drown, did he suffocate, did he fall over and break his leg? Was he alone or with others? All these questions must have eaten into her, just as they were doing now for him, thirty-nine years later.

For years he had tried to push the memory of his parents away. The only exception had been ten years earlier when a friend had told him about the Elisabeth Cross, a medal in recognition of those killed in any conflict to be awarded to the next of kin. Even then, he had decided against applying for it as if to be reminded of such pain in this way would be undignified, the process too painful.

"Why the cover-up?" was the question that bothered him most. Someone out there knew what happened. The government. Now middle-aged, he no longer believed a cover-up was as shocking or inconceivable as he once might have. He didn't have to think hard to find many examples of previous cover-ups by the government in recent years. There was the dodgy Iraq War of 2003 and the so-called weapons of mass destruction, a sign of how far politicians could lie or exaggerate if they felt entitled to do so. He also remembered the end of the Hillsborough Inquiry, the worst disaster in British sporting history, a tragic story of injustice, of cover-up, and collusion. The war itself had happened under unprecedented government media control. The few reporters allowed had been handpicked by the government, their reports scrutinised, censored, and delayed. Most of the final reports he had seen on YouTube were just voices embellished by still pictures. Most of the news had been leaked from London and image free for over two-thirds of the campaign.

One thing he did know was that Frank's theory about the SAS was clearly wrong. SAS selection was only for the best, the elite. To qualify for the SAS was the strictest process in the world, one that took years. There was no way, as Frank had claimed, that his dad just joined, whatever the circumstances. Rules were rules even in wartime. Furthermore, even if his father had been assisting the SAS in some capacity, that still didn't explain why no body was found.

Kevin already had a plan in place before they left for the islands to hire a lawyer to help him challenge the MOD and get them to reveal the details and start communication with veterans on Facebook, which was crammed with groups regarding the war and loads of veterans' profiles to interact with.

"Kev, come in, Kev! Make yourself at home," Frank beckoned as the door opened and Kevin walked inside.

Before long, Kevin was sitting in his usual chair, each man with a can of beer. Frank seemed in another pensive mood as he sat in his armchair and stared out of the open window.

"So, not long until we go, Frank. Are you excited?" Kevin said, eager to break the silence.

"No, not at all," Frank said without looking at him. "Actually, I am shitting myself. But I will manage. As long as it is still legal to drink beer, I shall be okay."

"Frank, there will be pubs everywhere! English pubs and English beer!"

"Then I shall survive," he said half-heartedly, finally turning his head to look at Kevin. "By the way, I'm sure you will be sick to death of me by the end of it."

"That's why I booked two single rooms. As long as we give each other space, it will be okay. I'll try to keep out of your way."

"I feel like a pill dispenser, Kev. I'm full of pills. My God, but truth is I'm still nervous. I find the prospect of flying halfway across the world daunting. It's a long way to travel, and I've never flown before."

Kevin disliked the way Frank kept being negative, but he decided to try ignoring his tone.

"Don't expect too much will you? You'll only get disappointed," Frank warned.

"I promise I will go there with an open mind, not expecting anything. At the very least, I will get to see where my dad spent his last moments. It will be worth it just to stand in the same places that he did."

"Yeah, I know that, but try to remember that for me, it won't be much fun."

Kevin was about to complain. Why was it so difficult to be positive from time to time, but he noticed that fear was now etched on Frank's face. Self-doubt filled his thoughts, and they hadn't even started the journey yet. Was Frank really ready for this?

"It won't be that bad, Frank..." was all he could think of to say. He sensed that a change in subject was needed, one that would hopefully cheer the old man up. "By the way, I've been looking on the internet a bit. I was wondering, what the hell is a craphat?"

His plan worked, for Frank started to laugh. "Oh, yes, that word brings back good memories. What a name, eh?"

"But what does it mean?" Kevin asked, encouraged by Frank's change in mood.

"It was used to describe anyone who wasn't a PARA. You see, a real PARA like your dad had a proper beret with a maroon colour."

"Oh, I see. Anyway, what else did they call you? Did you ever get called anything else?" Kevin asked, keen to keep Frank in a good mood.

"Oh, Kevin!" Frank chuckled, looking grateful for the question. "You would never guess some of the military slang."

"Go on then, tell me! "What were you called, apart from craphat?""

"A rear echelon motherfucker."

"Seriously? Are you kidding?" Kevin laughed.

"Not kidding. Rear echelon was the name for the support section, but they used to shorten it to REMF. So, I was called a fat REMF." Frank looked so happy as he turned towards

Kevin and made a grimace. "Oi, Drysdale, you fat REMF," he said like an actor on a stage, teasing his audience.

Kevin started to laugh. "Did they really call you that?" he said after calming down. "You're the last person I would call fat."

Much to Kevin's surprise, Frank stood up and mimicked, "You fat REMF, Drysdale, what are you?" He then mimicked answering in a childlike squeal. "I'm a fat REMF, *sir!*" as he stood to attention. Laughing more, he then sat down.

Kevin realised it was the first time he had ever heard Frank laugh in this way. Usually, jokes were one-liners followed by a quick cackle, but today he roared. However, as soon as he sat down, he looked very tired. The whole emotion of the day seemed to catch up with him, but Kevin decided they had come too far to stop now. It could take another month, if at all, to get this far again. The moment had arrived.

"Tell me something about my parents, Frank," Kevin asked, almost pleading.

"Well, it was my fault you were born!" Frank said.

"How do you mean?" Kevin asked, confused.

"Well, it was me who introduced your mum and dad. Back in the old days, when we hung out in Dundee, she was a friend of a friend, and I introduced them. They hit it off straight away. I remember when they began going out, they had this favourite song. It was like 'their' song."

"Really, what was it? Do you remember?"

"Yeah, it was a slow ballad by this group called Heatwave. 'Always and Forever,' it was."

"What?"

"You probably never heard of the song or the group, have you?"

"No, don't think so."

"Like I thought. Must be end of the seventies, I think. It's one of those slow love songs. I had forgotten about it, but then I heard it on the radio the other day. Jesus, music can be so powerful when it comes to memory. Just hearing the first few notes of that song brought back the memory of your mum and dad."

There was another long pause. Just like last time they had been in the pub and talking about the past, the atmosphere was electric, and Kevin prayed nobody would ring or knock on the door.

The more Kevin drank, the more he noticed Frank seemed troubled by something. Maybe it was the drinking, or something mentioned on the television. Whatever it was, Frank gradually seemed to curl up in a ball as if some memory had returned. He looked scared.

"What is it, Frank, tell me! What's stopping you? Talk to me."

"I don't know," Frank whispered, starting to stutter. "The truth," he said, taking a deep breath, "is that I'm scared."

"How do you mean? Scared of what?"

"It's scary that I don't remember anything. All this time and I still don't remember anything. I mean, what will happen when I do start to remember?"

"Well, maybe you'll see it wasn't as bad as you first thought?" Kevin said as thoughtfully as he could conjure.

"Yeah, but what if it is? What if it's much worse?"

"What if? Come on, Frank, it's stupid to think like that! You can't approach the past like that." Kevin stopped for a second, planning the next thing he would say. "Frank, why haven't you been before? A lot of veterans went back for the anniversaries and stuff. Why have you never been back?"

"Never been asked. Or maybe I was, but I just wanted to shut it out."

"Understandable. You refuse to look back, and every anniversary, every reminder is a nuisance, a pain. Is that right?"

"Something like that, yeah."

"But what about your old army friends?"

"I deliberately lost touch with them. I found it easier that way. I never wanted to talk to anyone about what happened. There were too many bad memories and all that, and there's nothing like an old face to remind you of the past, really."

"So, you felt that ignoring everything was the best way of coping?"

"Yeah. There's a reason why...why I never talked about it, Kev."

There was something strange about the atmosphere now. Kevin realised how much Frank had opened up to the best of his ability over the last few weeks. He had made such an effort, talking about impossible topics. The silence seemed to urge him to do the same.

"I think it's only fair that you know," Kevin said nervously.

"What do you mean?"

For a moment, Kevin thought about stopping, but the alcohol had loosened him up. "Frank, you have been very honest with me. I think it's only fair that I tell you. I know," he said softly.

"Kev, what are you talking about?"

"I know that you were shot."

Much to Kevin's surprise, Frank didn't look shocked or upset. Instead, he looked down embarrassed, not even bothering to deny it or ask how he had discovered the truth.

There was a long silence and then he looked away, saying, "Yeah, I don't want to go there."

"It's okay. You don't need to explain. Just thought you should know," Kevin said, noticing that Frank looked keen to change the subject quickly. He had had enough.

"I appreciate you telling me, Kevin, and I also want to thank you for paying for this trip."

"It's a pleasure, Frank."

"I know it's not all for me."

"What do you mean?"

"I mean, I know you want to find out about your dad. I promise I will help you with that as much as I can."

"That means a lot, Frank. I hope it helps you too, coming to terms with my dad and..."

"Yeah, but if I'm honest, I'm not just going back for your dad. I'm going back for my mum."

Kevin was shocked to hear Frank's words because it was the first time that he had mentioned Auntie Kay. In all the drama of the last month, Kevin had almost forgotten that Frank's mother had died.

"Well, that's part of why I am going back too, Frank," Kevin said in a hushed voice. "I'm going back for my mum."

Much to Kevin's annoyance, Frank waved his hand like he wasn't listening.

Kevin felt it was rude, unthoughtful, but he bit his lip and kept quiet. In the silence, he wondered how to be diplomatic. Then he said, "Think how proud Auntie Kay would be that you are going on this trip! She will be watching over you."

"Nah, I doubt it."

"Why not?" said Kevin, surprised. He looked at Frank and saw a very different Frank.

Frank closed his eyes shut, and straight away, Kevin had a terrible feeling that something bad was coming.

"I need to tell you this. You may not like it, but if we are going to go on holiday, I need to be honest. When I came home from the war, Auntie Kay never asked about what happened. She just wanted me to get better, and yet, I pushed her away for years. The only way I could get through the day was to get smashed out of my head just so I could forget. I became aggressive and violent. She started to nag me, said I had left a part of myself behind when I came home, that I wasn't the same person, that I was a shadow of myself. Each time she cried, I didn't care. I became emotionally cold and withdrawn. I pushed her away."

Frank shut his eyes and gulped in pain before he continued, "The lockdown was the final straw, Kev. I had nowhere to escape. When the pandemic came, I got so tired of the nagging. She got on my nerves so much, so I shut her out. I didn't really get it until it was too late, when she died. I took her for granted and then she was gone. Only now I realise that what I was doing was pushing her away and that I only hurt her more."

"What do you mean, Frank?" said Kevin.

Frank kept his eyes shut. "That night she died, I was half sleeping on the sofa with the TV on at the time. She had called out to me. I still vaguely remember her calling out for help. 'Frank,' she cried, but I was too drunk. It got on my nerves. 'Frank, Frank, help me, Frank.' I flipped. I shouted up the stairs, told her to shut the fuck up. She was annoying me, and her whining was interrupting my TV program. I even turned the volume up to drown her voice out. I didn't know she was begging for help. I thought she was just nagging me, as she always did."

It wasn't often you could hear the water flowing through the house, but in the deathly silence that followed Frank's admission, the pipes creaked and groaned. Kevin sat deathly still, frozen in shock.

"I must have fallen asleep on the sofa. When I woke up, it was light. I hadn't shut the curtains, and the bright light woke me. It was about nine in the morning or something. I could still hear her crying out. Upstairs. But her voice was weaker now. I ran up the stairs to see what was going on. Oh my God, she was lying on the floor. She had fallen over. She had obviously spent all night lying on the floor, calling me, crying out for help."

Kevin gasped.

Frank started to howl. "If I hadn't fobbed her off, she might have survived. She might have made it. I could have called for an ambulance, but no, I left her there to die. She only wanted the best for me, and yet I treated her so badly. I never realised how much I relied on her, how much I needed her. She always looked after me, cooked, cleaned, lent me money, put up with me. If I hadn't been drunk that night, maybe she wouldn't have died."

"Stop, Frank. Please," Kevin shouted.

But nothing could stop Frank now. " 'Why, Frankie? Why?' she said to me," he added quietly.

"What?" Kevin whispered.

" 'Why, Frankie? Why?' were the last words she said to me, Kevin. The last words she ever said. Before she died, as she lay on the floor, she said those words over and over again. 'Why, Frankie? Why?' " Frank fell silent, exhausted.

Kevin didn't know how to respond. He was horrified, wondering what he had let himself in for. So many lies. Now he understood how Auntie Kay had really died, and he was disgusted. His first reaction was to call off the trip. Frank was nothing more than a cold murderer. He felt so much anger. How dare he cause such a painful end? She hadn't deserved that. All he knew was that he had to get out. He needed time to think. He looked over to tell Frank that he was going, but he was already asleep on the sofa. He picked up his keys and left.

Chapter 15

Eyes still shut, Frank heard the door slam, but he didn't care. So what if Kevin was angry. It wasn't the first time. If Kevin never forgave him or cancelled the trip, what did it matter? All that mattered now was to get rid of the nightmares, to experience a night of peace.

As he lay there, he felt a strange feeling of release. He had told the truth, revealed his big secret, and as much as the truth hurt, he hoped that now maybe the nightmares would change. That was all he had ever wanted.

Fuck the trip. Fuck the pills. Just give me peace.

He began to feel the effects of the last pill he had taken while in the toilet. These were the sleeping pills he had been given by Dr. Price for the flight in a few days. He had only taken two, but that was enough. As he felt the earth disappear, he prayed for a nice dream.

Frank fell asleep straight away, and it seemed like his prayers had been answered for the nightmare was different again. Strangely, he was still in the same location, on the same hill, hiding behind the same jagged, deformed rock. On the same battlefield. Only this time, there was no sound. No mortar, no guns being fired, no tracers. No fierce wind. Only silence, as if the other side had surrendered.

The battle was over, and the sun was shining. The remnants of battle were everywhere, smoke and upturned rifles placed standing in the ground to indicate someone had died in these spots. He stood up, wondering if perhaps everyone was dead, because there was nobody around on the battlefield. Where was everyone? For a moment he wondered if perhaps he were dead and this was what hell looked like.

He was about to start walking up towards the rocky ridge when he heard a scuffling sound behind him. He turned around to his left and was shocked to see a moving body lying down on his back, his face turned towards him, staring straight at him, pleading.

As he moved closer, he realised it was his good friend, Baz. He looked so like Kevin there wasn't any doubt it was him. They shared the same features, the same expressive eyes and the same crooked nose, the big stocky build. Strangely, Baz looked younger than Kevin. Still a teenager, but his jaw was wider, his expression different. Baz had this curious look that was unique to him. His mouth curled slightly. Oddly, Baz wasn't in uniform but wearing blue jeans and a dirty white T-shirt as if he was about to head off down to the nearest pub in Aberdeen for a good night out.

Excited to see his old friend again, he ran towards him. He had so much to tell him. That he'd finally kept his promise, that he had taken good care of Kevin, that he missed him, that he wanted to take him to the pub. As he knelt down by his friend, he quickly realised he was not moving. Baz was dead. His eyes stared past him as if he weren't there.

Recoiling in horror, he moved back. As he did so, he clumsily hit Baz with his foot and his left arm moved on the ground. It was then he saw Baz's left hand was open and in the middle of his palm was a silver necklace, glinting in the moonlight. Curious, he picked it up from Baz's cold lifeless hand. He held the necklace up to the light and examined it closer. It looked dirty and unpolished, but the silver still managed to glint. It was a half-heart pendant. Part of a two necklace set, each with half of the same heart. And when the two heart pieces were finally reunited and placed back together, the heart would be whole again.

He remembered it now. This was the necklace Baz had been wearing the last time he saw him on the MV *Norland*, after they had arrived on the Falkland Islands. He remembered seeing it catch the light when Baz leaned over to pick up his backpack while getting ready to go ashore.

He wiped the dirt off it with his sleeve and then strained his eyes to read the inscription. It was then he noticed the two half hearts had been reunited. The last time he had seen the pendant, it had been only one-half of the heart. Now it was symbolically whole again.

Frank read the inscription engraved across both halves. "Angie & Baz, Always & Forever."

RECONSTRUCTION

Chapter 16

After over twenty hours of flying, Frank woke up to the sounds of the seatbelt sign warning and the pilot announcing the plane was now approaching its destination. Immediately, he was overwhelmed with panic and trepidation. It had been thirty-nine years since the last time he'd come here. Back then, he had not arrived onboard a luxury jet airliner but crammed into an old roll-on/roll-off car ferry, part of a British task force, as it ploughed tentatively eight thousand miles across the icy rough seas of the South Atlantic. He had been a different person back then, a naïve teenager full of dreams and hope, unprepared for the events that were about to unfold. What was he really expecting to achieve by revisiting these barren, weather-beaten islands, and what effect would returning have on his nightmares? Just as he had predicted, the dreams had changed again. This time, his dead mother had been replaced by his dead friend Baz holding a necklace in his hand.

What did the dream mean? Logically, it made little sense. The two parts of the necklace had been joined together, but if the necklace had really existed, both Baz and Angie would have had their own half-heart pendant. That was the whole point of it, the romantic notion of reuniting. So, if he had seen Baz wearing it that day on the ship, he would have only seen one-half of the necklace.

His thoughts were distracted by the sudden movements of other passengers straining to see out the windows and curiosity got the better of him. He took a deep breath, put his face against the window, and peered down. As he saw the archipelago through the thin spray of clouds below, he gasped. It all looked so different from how he remembered. He could not recall the sun ever shining, but today it seemed to strut its rays, proudly revealing a landscape filled with nature and wildlife, dominated by bright green grass and large cascades of rocks that swept down the hillsides. The dark sea where so many had lost their lives was now a light blue colour, its waves gently pounding the white sandy beaches.

It was then he knew it had been a mistake to return. Time had changed everything. These islands were no longer the dark, inhospitable, unfriendly, barren wastelands he remembered but a wealthy tourist mecca. Down below were graveyards and cemeteries, but the war was no longer on these islands. These islands were not the enemy—the enemy was his mind.

As the seatbelt sign flashed on again and the plane began its final approach, Frank felt more alone than he had ever felt before. Even as the plane touched down safely on the runway, he already wanted to turn back and go home.

Chapter 17

As Kevin lay on his hotel room bed in Port Stanley, he smiled with relief. It had now been five days since they arrived on the Falkland Islands. Today, quarantine was over and he was finally free to go wherever he wanted.

Admittedly, stranded in a posh hotel for five days was hardly the worst place to be in quarantine. There was so much to see from his hotel room window, like glorious sunset views and the shipwrecks from the nearby Stanley Harbour. He loved the smell of the fresh Antarctic air, and the sounds of birds amidst the roar of the wind that rattled his hotel window.

Sipping his coffee, he reminisced about how the journey itself had gone very smoothly. His biggest fear, that he would be stuck with a whining Frank, had not materialised. Instead, he seemed quite content to be left alone, keeping himself busy or sleeping. Perhaps he was feeling guilty and embarrassed about what he had told him about Auntie Kay.

He was relieved he had not given in to the temptation of cancelling the whole trip. He had been so angry that day at Frank's house, listening to the guy telling him how Auntie Kay had died. She had deserved so much better, but so much money had been spent on this trip and he was unwilling to cancel the once in a lifetime opportunity to trace his dad's last steps.

Fortunately, keeping his distance from Frank had been made easier by the unforeseen appearance of a new friend. One of the fellow passengers on the special bus that drove them from the airport to Port Stanley was a local islander called Jack Jennings, who had been visiting relatives abroad. He and Frank had really hit it off, Jack clearly impressed that he was a Falklands veteran and accordingly was now treating Frank like he was royalty.

Jack's arrival had also left Kevin free to focus on researching his dad's disappearance in more detail. Before setting out from home, he had hired a lawyer to investigate what rights he had concerning access to information from the Ministry of Defence. He wanted to know why his father was declared MIA, where he might have gone before he went missing and if there were other details that could be uncovered that might solve the mystery. Above all, he wanted to know why the government appeared unwilling to divulge the truth about what happened.

The most likely explanation so far was not, as Frank had claimed, that he had joined the SAS but that his injuries were far more serious than first thought and he was sent to the medical ship, the SS *Uganda*, fifty miles from the islands. Kevin had discovered that the Geneva convention—an agreement of international humanitarian law that defined how the wounded and sick were treated in war—stated that, once someone was sent to the hospital ship with an injury, they were unable to return to the combat zone. It didn't matter how serious the injury was, to be on that ship meant your involvement in the war was effectively over. Therefore, if he could prove that his father had been treated on the medical ship, then it meant he could not have disappeared on the islands. He had also read that, if his father had been on the SS *Uganda*, it was probable that he had been transported to Montevideo, in Uruguay, where he would have been flown back to the UK.

He had also taken the plunge and begun looking for veterans on Facebook who could help him. So far, conversations had been polite chat, but one in particular, David Townsend, remembered his father well and had started to ask around and would be getting back in touch when he found out more.

But for now, Kevin was looking forward to experiencing the islands. Tomorrow they were scheduled for an early start, a two-hour drive to Darwin and Goose Green. The plan was to walk from near Camilla Creek, the starting point of the battle, to Goose Green. Once tomorrow was over, they were free agents. Apart from a stay in Darwin tomorrow night, the rest of the trip would be spent in the capital. Kevin already had plans to take a wildlife tour to see the penguins and birds. Most of all, he was keen to retrace his father's footsteps in San Carlos, maybe take a trip up the Sussex Mountains, or visit the Ajax Bay hospital, the last possible location of his father before disappearing.

Yes, this was going to be one hell of a trip. He was excited at the prospect of finally making peace with what happened to his father, that the mysteries of the last forty years could now be solved.

Chapter 18

As Frank sat in the corner of the Victory Bar, he couldn't remember the last time he had been so happy. In this bar, the locals treated him like royalty and bought all his beers, and it hadn't taken him long to settle in. It also helped that nobody on these islands wore a face mask, something that made him feel quite liberated.

The original plan had been to spend the day walking around the capital with his new friend, Jack Jennings, but he was quickly distracted by the sign on the side of a house on which was written Victory Bar. Initially, he found it hard to believe this was a bar. The building's dark brown wooden exterior with a green wooden roof to match made it look more like a house. But once inside, it was more British than any pub he had ever seen. The ceiling was adorned with thousands of union jack flags, complemented by the fish and chips menu, the pool table, and the television on the wall playing the Sky Sports channel.

Smiling, he recalled how Jack had saved the whole trip from disaster. Things between he and Kevin had been awkward on the journey over, and he had been pessimistic about what lay ahead on arrival. Then, despite being in quarantine himself, Jack had gone out of his way to make Frank's stay as pleasant as possible, even tipping some of the staff in his hotel to ensure he got everything he wanted. Nothing was too much trouble.

Jack was a bit older and had been brought up in a farming community outside of Port Stanley but now lived in the capital, taking advantage of the lucrative tourist trades. He was exactly how Frank had expected an islander to look, with casual clothes and unkempt hair.

His thoughts were interrupted by a tap on his shoulder.

"So, Frank, you'd rather stay here, right?" Jack asked. "You don't want to see the liberation memorial?"

"No, I'll have plenty of time to see that. To be honest, it's just nice to be in a pub again. Feels like weeks with the long journey over here and all the quarantine."

"Quite understand. Oh, hang on," Jack said, excitedly waving someone over. "Frank," he said proudly, "I want you to meet my neighbour, Fiona Harvey."

Frank turned around to see the biggest smile he had ever seen. She was a pretty, slim girl of medium height, with black curly hair, and glorious big blue eyes. For a second, he wondered if she had mistaken him for someone else.

"Hi, Frank!" she almost shouted with excitement. Even before he had the chance to answer, she was quickly explaining that she was not only Jack's neighbour but also his work assistant. She spoke breathlessly, telling him she had heard so much about him and how she had really been looking forward to meeting him.

At first, Frank felt awkward. He was not used to such forwardness or so much attention. As she asked politely about how the trip had been so far, he noticed she was wearing tight blue jeans and a multicoloured sweater. If he had to guess, he would say she looked somewhere around forty years old.

"Oh, Frank, you're drinking a Longdon Pride. Do you like it? My favourite is the Rock Hopper. You must try them all." She gasped, her big blues eyes looking at him adoringly.

"Yes," Frank said, returning the smile. The barman had already told him the local beers all made references to the islands and this was a location he knew about, another battle of the war.

As their conversation continued, he became fascinated by her outgoing, flirty character and the way she nervously laughed at anything he said. He sensed a vulnerability hidden behind her smile that he found endearing. He suspected her enthusiasm was due to him being a Falklands veteran, but right now, he didn't care. His first proper day on the islands and already the attention he was getting from the islanders, especially this attractive woman, made him feel more alive than he had for years. Unfortunately, she was not able to stay long.

"I'm sorry, Frank, but I have to go back to work. Hope to see you again." She then gave him a hug and was gone.

Frank's eyes followed her slim body all the way to the nearby exit.

"Wow, she liked you," said Jack.

"What the fuck was that?" Frank gasped, still in shock.

"One of the nicest people I know...heart of gold."

"Quite nice to look at too," said Frank sheepishly.

Jack laughed. "She's a real islander. Her family stretches back for centuries. One thing you will come to understand, Frank, is how much we islanders feel grateful to veterans like you."

"Well, I don't feel like I deserve it, Jack. I didn't do that much, you know?"

"Everybody did their little bit, Frank! Just remember, there aren't so many tourists around as there usually are."

"What do you mean?"

Jacked winked at Frank. "Well, the pandemic has hit tourism, so maybe we are desperate!" He laughed loudly and patted Frank on the back. "Just kidding, Frank."

Frank smiled back, appreciating how Jack's humour stopped the mood from changing.

"Anyway, I've got to go," he said looking at his watch. "Got to catch up with the work and stuff."

"No problem, Jack. Thanks for showing me around this morning."

"It was a pleasure, Frank. I would have liked to stay longer, but..."

"Sure, Jack, I'll be fine."

"So, tomorrow, you are off to Goose Green, right?"

"Yeah," Frank sighed. "Dreading it to be honest."

"Okay, if I don't see you today, we can meet after the trip. Hope it goes well," he said, patting him again on the back. "Don't forget to call me if I can help."

As soon as Jack left, Frank felt anxious. Maybe it was the reminder of tomorrow's trip. Maybe it was something to do with feeling so happy. For so long, being happy had made him feel guilty, that he didn't deserve to be alive and content. His thoughts turned to Baz, how he would have loved to be here with him, having a beer, drinking with and being looked after by the friendly islanders, and being chatted up by flirty pretty girls.

Admittedly, the new nightmare had been bothering him —stuck in quarantine for five days had given him plenty of time to contemplate on his life. What did the dream really mean? How could Baz's face seem so fresh in his memory?

And the necklace Baz had been holding, was it really a "two half-heart pendant" necklace or had his imagination got carried away? He was pretty sure that Baz had been wearing it last time they had met on the *Norland*.

Kevin. He had almost forgotten about him. He had hardly seen him since they arrived five days earlier. Maybe Kevin might know something about the necklace? They weren't on great terms at the moment, but they would be off on a trip together tomorrow. Someone had to make the first move.

Excited, he picked up his mobile and called him.

Chapter 19

Kevin was on an evening walk when Frank called. Normally he would have dreaded a call from him, but right now he was in a good mood. Even at eight in the evening, he felt calmed by the beautiful red sunset, the colours and intensity of the light like an inspirational fire in the sky.

He had just spent an enjoyable day walking around the capital. There was so much to see in the quaint hillside town, with its tiny two and a half thousand population. One of the highlights had been a visit to Christchurch Cathedral, one of the capital's best-known landmarks with its huge whalebone arch monument in the front of the building.

Ironically, everywhere he looked, he saw reminders of home—red phone boxes, cars driving on the left side of the road, the English currency, and yet it was also very different. The town was so tiny it could have almost fit on just one street in Dundee, the houses looked like little Lego constructions, and there were no cash points, advertising billboards, or traffic lights.

Frank had asked him if he wanted to meet him at the Victory. It felt childish to still be holding grievances against him. Besides, he was well aware that tomorrow they would be travelling together. It seemed best to enjoy the holiday-like atmosphere while it lasted, so he'd agreed to Frank's suggestion.

On arrival, he hardly recognised his adoptive father sitting in the corner of the bar, surrounded by laughing people. Usually, the sight of Frank in a bar was depressing, but today his smile was infectious. As the evening progressed, Kevin discovered Frank could be a different person, in a holiday mood, free of the worries that had tormented him for so long. Here they were equals, no longer Frank's adopted son. They relaxed and chatted with the locals and played darts. He was no longer the weak, feeble, nervous character Kevin was used to. Kevin wondered that perhaps Dr. Price had been right after all, that this trip was the best medicine for Frank. But it was hard not to wonder what it would be like tomorrow, when they would be visiting the battlefields.

After an hour of playing pool, watching sports on the television, and chatting with the locals, it was nearly eleven o'clock. Suddenly they were alone, sitting in a quiet corner, with only the noise of the barmen cleaning up. Much to Frank's amusement, drinking times on these islands were the same as back in the UK.

"Eight thousand miles away, you'd think the people could stay open a bit longer." Frank chuckled. "Seriously, Kev, I love it here. I'm so glad we came, and I will try my best to help you find out what happened to your dad."

"Don't think about that now, Frank," Kevin said, unprepared for the change in subject. "It's just good to see you happy."

"I feel I have one thing to do while I'm over here," Frank said. "I mean, I realised it today. I'm not really here to find out what happened to me. I mean, screw my memory, screw the problems I've had. What matters is that I'm here.

Being able to be here in person and show my respect to all my fellow soldiers who died here, that's what matters. If I don't remember what really happened here, then it doesn't matter. I just want to be able to kneel and pray and show my respect, say goodbye to your dad. Yeah, that's why I've come."

"Frank, were you in Port Stanley last time?" Kevin asked, instinctively.

Frank no longer displayed the awkward body language of old, the stuttered nervous talking, no fear of retaliation or angry responses. It just seemed natural to ask, especially as Frank had mentioned his father first. "No, never been here. When I was shot, I guess I must have been flown straight to Ajax Bay, right?"

"Where Dad was?" Kevin woke up, shocked that Frank had not mentioned this before. Had Frank seen his father there, he wondered.

"I know what you're thinking, Kevin. You're wondering if I saw your dad?"

"Well, yeah...sort of?"

"I told you before. I never saw your dad after we said goodbye on the *Norland*. Besides, you need to remember if I had been sent to Ajax Bay, it would have happened a few weeks after your dad. He would have long disappeared by the time I arrived."

Kevin nodded. After a few minutes of silence, he felt brave enough to ask another question. "So, do you remember what happened when you got home?"

"Yeah, when your mum died not long after, I knew I had to take care of you."

"Of course. So, you left the army, right?"

"Yeah, I got a PVR, a Premature Voluntary Release. I filled in some forms, and they worked out how much they owed me from my rank and stuff. Was a pittance, mind you? I didn't get much as I had only been in the army about ten months or something."

"Okay."

"Kevin, can I ask you something?" Frank said in a low voice.

"Sure, what about?" He noticed Frank looked heavy in thought, a look he hadn't seen for a while. He had a bad feeling.

"Well, it's something...it's just... Well, the thing is, that time on the *Norland*, you know when I last saw him..."

"Yes?"

"Well, I remembered recently that he was wearing a silver necklace."

"A silver necklace?" Kevin replied, a little worried where this conversation was heading. Was Frank drunker than he looked? Had he sneaked off to the bathroom and taken a pill? It was late now, and it was a big day tomorrow. All of a sudden, he wanted this strange conversation to finish.

"Yeah," Frank said, still looking straight at Kevin. "I remembered it in the last few weeks. It was one of those half-heart pendants ones. You know, really it was two necklaces, and when separated, each necklace had a half heart," said Frank using his fingers to demonstrate what he meant. "It's kind of a romantic thing. What couples do when they are apart, right?"

"I think I get what you mean, but why are you telling me this?"

"Well, I just wanted to ask you if you remember a necklace like that?"

"Me? What do you mean?"

"Well, you know, maybe your mum left you it when she died?"

"Frank, I wasn't even one year old when they died!"

"I know, but maybe they left you something in a will or you found something when you were growing up?"

"No, I don't know about any necklace. I'm pretty sure anyway," Kevin replied. As far he could remember, all he had from his parents were a few photos of the wedding and a couple of his dad in uniform. Maybe there were a few wine glasses he inherited but certainly nothing that resembled a necklace.

"Sorry I asked, Kev. I was just curious, that's all."

Kevin felt guilty seeing the pain on Frank's face. It was so unlike him to say sorry. "You really don't think it means anything do you, Frank?"

"I don't know. I remembered it recently in a dream and was wondering what happened to it."

"A dream?" Kevin asked, wondering if he meant nightmare.

"Yeah."

"So, what do you remember about it?"

"The inscription on it."

"Oh? What was it?" Kevin asked, now curious.

"Baz and Angie, Always and Forever."

"Oh, right!" Kevin said, surprised by how sure Frank seemed. He remembered a few months ago back in Tayport, Frank telling him some story about his mum and dad's song, some slow ballad he had never heard of, called "Always and Forever" from the seventies. "That was their song, right?"

"Yeah..." Suddenly Frank let out a big laugh. "Yeah, you're right Kevin, this is silly, isn't it? Let's go back to the hotel and get some sleep."

A relieved Kevin looked on as Frank went to the bar to thank the bar staff. Once again, he was reminded how gregarious and friendly Frank could be. He had noticed this evening how endearing and friendly and helpful islanders were, especially to Frank, how they all seemed to go out of their way to make him feel welcome, even refusing to take his money for the beers. Was that why Frank seemed such a different person, he wondered, because people were acting so nice towards him? It brought out the best in him, or was it the new surroundings? A welcome departure from the humdrum of daily life back home?

As they walked down the now dark and empty streets to the hotel, Kevin marvelled at Frank's cheerful optimism as he sang the song hopelessly out of tune.

"Always and forever, each moment with you, is just like a dream to me, that somehow came true."

He had to admit the song was nice, but he had not heard it before and made a mental note to listen to the original and better sung version on Spotify.

After saying goodbye to Frank in the reception, Kevin went up to his room and got ready for bed. As his head hit the pillow, he knew it wouldn't take long before he fell asleep.

He grabbed his headphones and found the song on his mobile and listened carefully to the song. Thanks to Frank's awful recital outside, he knew he had found the right version. It was a song by a group called Heatwave, a slow soul record. He had certainly never heard it before, but as he listened, he imagined his mum and dad, young teenagers, dancing together to the song on the dance floor. It was the first time he had ever been able to picture them in his mind and was surprised to feel a tear fall down his cheek. It was a confirmation of their existence. His last thought as he closed his eyes was that he was proud he had paid for the holiday. It had completely changed Frank already. He hoped the new Frank was here to stay, that his good mood would last.

Yeah, this trip might not be so bad after all...

Chapter 20

As Frank lay in his hotel bed, he hoped the sleeping pill he had taken ten minutes earlier would soon start working. It was going to be a long day tomorrow, and he needed to get up early for the ride to Darwin.

It had been an amazing day, such a long journey, full of laughter and tears, and then a wonderful evening. He hadn't bought a beer all day. Today had made him realise he had so much to look forward to. He had a good friend in Jack and was finally on good terms with Kevin.

Most of all, he was hopeful he would see that girl Fiona again. There was something about her even though he knew it was too good to be true. He tried to tell himself not to get his hopes up and he was only here for a couple of weeks anyway. Even if she did like him, perhaps she already had a boyfriend. Perhaps she was only giving him attention because he was a veteran. Maybe she was nice to him because Jack was his friend, and she wanted to make him feel comfortable and welcome.

Whatever the reason was, she had certainly succeeded in getting his full attention. Just in a few minutes, she had managed to knock him off his perch and confuse him with warm, basic feelings of human need. That smile, that look of interest, it had been decades since a pretty girl smiled at him.

But alone and tired, it didn't take long for his thoughts to darken. Travelling eight thousand miles away was not going to stop his dreams. The last dream still worried him. It had been bothering him since he got here. He had not told Kevin the whole dream on purpose. It seemed insensitive to mention that his dad was dead or that it had taken place at Darwin. But the more he thought about it, the more it bothered him. That's why he had asked Kevin about the necklace. He was aware Kevin might ridicule the dream, being the cynical kind, the type who found analysing dreams as pointless as reading the shape of tea leaves in a teacup. Dreams were just the imagination. But to give him credit, Kevin had listened without judging.

The main reason he had wanted to discuss it with Kevin was because, if the necklace really did exist, then it also might provide a clue as to what happened to Baz. Did Baz find a way to send his piece of necklace heart back home to his wife? Were the two bits of heart ever reunited in real life? Or did Baz die still wearing it? If somebody knew where the necklace was, it might provide a clue as to his last resting place. Besides, what if someone had stumbled across it and reported it? Maybe in the decades since the war, somebody had found it on another island where the SAS had operated. Yes, he had concluded, the necklace was an important clue to the location of the body, and he would start asking the islanders about it tomorrow.

He began to feel drowsy and knew sleep was not far off. Desperate to distract his thoughts, he got out of bed, walked to the open hotel window and breathed in the strong sea air. Unlike earlier, the wind was now the only noise coming from the street below. No town chatter, and only flickering lights in a cloud of darkness.

Tomorrow would be hard. They were going to Darwin, retracing the Battle of Goose Green. For years he had dreamed about the rock on Darwin Ridge, where they had been ambushed and where the phosphorous grenade had exploded, and the burning enemy body had rolled down. Tomorrow, he would finally come face to face with this hill and sit once again behind the rock that had saved his life. He would never forget that rock, it had such a special shape. It had probably aged and changed colour, but it was symbolic too. He would finally be able to close this chapter of his life, to bury it once and for all.

As he leaned out of the window, he got this feeling of déjà vu. The sun had long descended into the horizon, yet there was something that niggled at him. He couldn't put his finger on what it was, but something seemed familiar. He had never been to Port Stanley, he was certain. Perhaps it was because he was so far away from home. Was it the view, the sea air, or was it the wind? That niggling feeling started to subside as he shut the curtains and got back into his bed.

As he fell asleep, he found himself taking cover behind the same rock at Darwin. There was no mistaking its coarse texture and distinctive shape. Unlike his recent dream, the battle was underway again. Artillery and shells zinged past him as mortars and grenades exploded all around. He dared not look to his right where he knew the dead body was. Whether it was his mother or Baz's voice waiting to frighten him was no longer his main concern. All he knew was that the longer he remained stuck behind this rock, the more likely he would be shot.

He decided to make a run for it, blindly grabbing his SMG as he stood and bolted up the hill. In the blind panic to find safe ground, he failed to see the bunker right ahead of him and fell into it. It wasn't deep enough to injure him, but as he came to his senses, he realised he was in an enemy bunker. About a metre away from where he had fallen in, he saw an enemy soldier crumpled up against some rocks, half lying on the ground and shivering in the cold air. He noticed the soldier's leg was torn off, but he was still alive, severely wounded and in obvious agony. The man's white eyes looked like the moon, and he stared at Frank.

"*Por favor*...please," the soldier whined. "Please, *gracias*." He sounded like a cornered rat with no option but to beg for mercy.

It was then Frank noticed the pistol lying by his side. He tried to think straight, to do the right thing, but his heart was pumping with adrenaline. The noise and flashes of combat had him on edge. What mattered was that he had the advantage, for it was his machine gun that was pointing at the enemy.

He couldn't take the chance, so he fired.

It jammed.

It only took a tenth of a second to decide what he had to do next. Instinct took over. Something he had learnt on the drills on the journey over. "If you're having difficulty with thick clothing," they had told him, "Go through the eye..."

The bayonet on his SMG glistened in the moonlight as he plunged it forward towards the face of the enemy.

This was the moment Frank woke up struggling to understand where he was, his screams piercing his ears. He thought he saw Baz's body hunched over him, screaming at him to wake up, but after a few seconds he realised it was Kevin standing over him, looking terrified.

"Wake up, Frank. For fuck's sake!" Kevin was shouting at him. "Wake up!"

Chapter 21

"What the fuck were you dreaming about last night?" Kevin asked as he sat opposite Frank in the restaurant, eating breakfast.

"Not now," Frank replied, embarrassed.

"But, Frank—"

"I'll tell you another time, Kevin," he said quietly, gazing out of the window, trying to pretend nothing had happened. "Not now."

Hours earlier, Kevin had been fast asleep when he was awakened by loud screaming. His first thought as he sprang out of bed was that the noise was coming from somewhere outside, on the street. It was only when he ran out of his room that he realised the screams were coming from Frank's room next door. As he banged on the door to no avail, the hotel manager had appeared from downstairs, curious as to what was going on. After a brief explanation, he quickly unlocked the door and let Kevin in.

It took a few minutes to wake Frank up. He seemed to be possessed, his arms and legs lashing out at the air as if in self-protection. Trying to shake him out of his nightmare or shouting back at him achieved little. It was only when the manager turned on the main room light that Frank's eyes, dazed by the bright light, finally flicked open.

Even then, it was still not over.

"Baz, Baz," he had whispered softly. "Please..."

"Wake up, Frank. For fuck's sake!" Kevin had shouted at him. "It's me, Kevin. Wake up!"

When Frank finally came around, the hotel room filled with welcoming silence that reminded Kevin he had witnessed these outbursts before. He recalled decades earlier, as a small child, lying awake on his bed and hearing loud screaming coming from Frank's bedroom. This was always followed by the sound of creaking floorboards as Auntie Kay got out of bed and raced across the landing. On one occasion, he had been daring enough to climb out of bed and peep through the ajar door of Frank's bedroom, watching puzzled as Auntie Kay fought to wake him up.

"Frank, we can always do this trip another time?" Kevin asked, trying to sound positive.

It didn't seem fair that he should miss this one opportunity to visit one of the places where his father had walked. He was also well aware of the hard work and planning that had gone into today's outing. Tour guides normally catered for groups of tourists, but today, one had been privately booked to drive them both to Camilla Creek. It was an hour and a half drive from Port Stanley, and on arrival, the guide would then personally escort them as they walked to Darwin three miles away, retracing the steps taken by 2 PARA at the Battle of Goose Green. They would then stay the rest of day and night relaxing at Darwin house, a luxury guesthouse set in the picturesque setting of Darwin Settlement.

"No, Kev. I have to do this. I have to go," he said almost in a whisper, aghast at the suggestion.

"You sure?"

"Yeah, when today's over, I can take it easy here in Stanley."

After a quiet breakfast, there was more bad news waiting for Kevin. As he packed his suitcase, he noticed an email on his mobile sent from his lawyer back in the UK. The Ministry of Defence had written to confirm that Baz Turner had died in the Falklands conflict. As no remains or grave had been positively identified, his casualty classification was given as MIA, or Missing in Action. The ministry also confirmed they were in possession of details concerning his last known location but that it was not in the "public inter-est" to reveal them. The lawyer ended the email by writing he was going to put pressure on the ministry to reveal these details under the terms of the Freedom of Information Act.

Though he had been expecting this news, it still confused him. His dad had been a young private, not a high-ranking leader with access to secret information. So much time had passed since the end of the war, it seemed there were no secrets left that needed keeping. Top secret missions such as the Black Buck raids, the real position of the Belgrano when it was sunk, the disclosure that nuclear weapons had been onboard British submarines and the secret inquiry into the sinking of HMS *Sheffield* had all been declassified and were in the public domain. So why the reluctance to share his father's last whereabouts? Hadn't his family suf-fered enough?

Fortunately, it was not all bad news. There was a lovely Facebook message from his new contact, Dave Townsend, who had promised to do some investigating into his father's background. This morning, he had messaged Kevin with some feedback on his enquiries.

Kevin was shocked to learn that there was another paratrooper called "Baz" in 2 PARA, and this name similarity had led to a lot of confusion. Dave also warned that his father wasn't the only person who had gone missing in the Falklands War. There was the famous story about Scots Guardsman Phillip Williams who had been injured at the battle of Mount Tumbledown and went missing for seven weeks before turning up at Bluff Cove. Apparently, he had been wandering around confused and disoriented, living in caves, surviving on Argentine ration packs. Of course, this person had survived whereas his dad hadn't, but Dave hoped there may be some clues in that story. Then there was the guy who had been captured, Flight Lieutenant Jeffrey Glover, one of only two British prisoners taken by Argentina in the Falklands War. Apparently, the day he was captured, he was found with a dislocated shoulder, but that day, he still agreed to a blood transfusion to keep a wounded Argentine alive.

Kevin's thoughts were disturbed by the ringing of his mobile. It was a text message to tell him the taxi was ready and waiting for them in the reception.

Chapter 22

As the taxi drove out of Port Stanley, Frank no longer felt apprehensive about what the day would bring. He had come prepared. The medication he had taken this morning was now working, and the sense of calm it gave him was reassuring. He checked his right jacket pocket again, finding the small bottle of whisky he had bought last night was there just in case of an emergency. In the front passenger seat of the black Land Rover, Kevin was busy chatting to the guide, occasionally glancing into the rearview mirror to check if he was okay.

Alone in the back seat, he leaned back and gathered his thoughts. As he had feared, returning to these islands had dramatically affected his nightmares. After years of dreaming about his dead mother at Darwin Hill, his dreams had finally started to veer off in different directions. Little splinters of his memory were now returning and he had opened his own personal Pandora's box of horrors.

As if the new dream about Baz and the necklace had not been enough to bear, last night, he had dreamt about bayoneting an enemy soldier. He wondered if his brain had made that up, or if he had bayonetted someone. He certainly had no recollection of it. He knew dreams were neither factual retellings nor interpretations of real events.

He also knew his previous dream about a dead Baz holding his necklace on Darwin Hill made no sense because the facts were that Baz had survived the Battle of Goose Green, suffered from grenade shrapnel and ended up at Ajax Bay. It was also a fact that he had not seen Baz since the day 2 PARA embarked at San Carlos.

Even an amateur analysis of his dreams could spot other discrepancies. Why was he always alone? What happened to the other stretcher bearers he had set off with? He was not a frontline soldier, so how had he ended up in an enemy bunker? Most jarring of all, the enemy he had bayonetted in the dream last night had a pistol, but it could not have been the one that shot him because he was shot at Wireless Ridge nearly one hundred miles away, in a battle that had taken place nearly two weeks later!

The real problem seemed to be his self-confidence. He was too insecure to be certain of anything. That was why, after the initial shock of the new nightmare had worn off this morning, Frank realised that starting to remember the past might actually be a good thing. Perhaps on this journey of discovery, he would get the answers that had eluded him for so long. Finally, the truth seemed within his reach.

Most importantly, all of his nightmares had one thing in common. There were all based at the same location, Darwin Ridge. The ridge the burnt enemy body had rolled down, the ridge where the dead Baz had held his necklace in his hand, and the ridge where he had bayonetted the enemy soldier. All of these incidents had occurred after he lay down hiding behind the rock, ambushed and in fear for his life.

Yes, the rock. The very rock that had saved his life, shielding him from the enemy as he lay there alone and confused. The rock was the key, the link to recovering his memory. Today he would find the rock and his memory would return and then he would finally be able to put the past behind him. This trip to Darwin had now become a crusade to find the truth.

He was curious what the rock would look like. For years it had probably been battered about by wind, snow, and rain. Most likely it was now a different colour. Perhaps it was now covered in newly grown moss, dirt, and bird faeces. But one thing he did know, its shape would be unchanged. The unique shape that made it so distinctive in his dreams. Thirty-nine years had passed, but he would find it.

Chapter 23

As the Land Rover drove into the field near Camilla Creek, Kevin recognised the area straight away. Compared with his previous scrutiny of the place online, it was exactly as he had expected—wet and drizzly with low, treeless tussock-covered hills. In the middle of the nearest field, about five hundred yards away, lay the famous shepherd's house, a small privately-owned cottage from where the battle had started in the darkness.

It had been an interesting journey. Apart from driving on the left side, roads were so different compared to back home. There were no traffic lights, traffic jams or angry impatient drivers. Only quiet, narrow, and winding roads stretching out in front of them. Frank, sitting quietly in the backseat of the four-seater Land Rover, had not posed any problems. Instead, he had been remarkably calm considering the circumstances.

He also found the guide very friendly and informative. A proud native islander, his family could be traced back at least six generations to these islands. Now in his thirties, he made his living catering to tourists who arrived in the summer season from the cruise ships in Port Stanley, ferrying them around in a bus on battle tours or nature trips to see the renowned wildlife. Kevin had politely informed him of the sensitive nature of today's trip and been reassured to hear that many veterans had returned here over the years and that the guide had personally helped many of them on their journey of rediscovery.

But as Kevin stepped out of the car, he was taken by surprise and suddenly overcome with emotion. As the cold wind blew against his face, he realised that, for the first time ever, he was now walking in his father's footsteps. He was now near the starting line of the Battle of Goose Green, where his father had helped fight the enemy to submission before succumbing to shrapnel injuries.

The tears came quickly. He thought of all the years he had spent wondering what his parents were like, what sort of life he may have had if they had still been alive. Many a time alone in his bed, he had wondered what might have happened to him if his dad had not been killed. Would his parents still be together? He might have had a good up-bringing instead of the chaotic, stressful one with Frank and Auntie Kay. He knew it was pointless to think like this, but today he had no resistance to the emotions of the occasion.

He had been informed yesterday that today's trip would require extra clothing. This may have been summer season, but in the open land, the infamous and relentless Antarctic wind of the islands were in full force. The land ahead also reliably difficult terrain in places, wet and soggy. Once all the protective clothing was on and they were ready to head off, Kevin turned his attention to Frank, still putting on his mountain boots. Walking over, he noticed Frank looked tired and exhausted, clearly also struggling with the emotional challenge of being back here.

"You okay, Frank? It's your day, you decide the pace. There's no rush. We have all day to get to Darwin."

"Kev, I remember the cottage over there," he said, pointing in the distance. "Even though last time it was pitch dark…"

"Okay, but are you ready?" Kevin asked again impatiently, sparing a thought for the guide waiting patiently in the distance.

"Kev, look, I don't want to walk with the guide. I would prefer to be alone. I can walk a few steps behind you. Hope you don't mind. I just need to take it all in, you know?"

"Sure, Frank." Kevin smiled but inside he felt frustrated. He was sure the reason was so that Frank could secretly sip from his whisky flask in his pocket. For a selfish moment, he wished he could have experienced today alone, free of the responsibility of looking after Frank. He longed to see for himself the places where his father had been, but today was Frank's trip.

But there were also many questions he hoped to ask Frank as they walked together across the fields, questions the guide certainly had no hope of answering. Which direction had his father gone that day, and where had he been treated for shrapnel? From where would he have been evacuated to Ajax Bay?

As the walk to Darwin Ridge and Goose Green finally got underway, Kevin walked with the guide a few yards ahead of Frank as agreed. The wind was behind them today, and talking meant shouting to be heard. As he chatted with the guide, Kevin learnt that Darwin was named after Charles Darwin, the great explorer and father of the theory of evolution who visited the place in 1833 on his second voyage aboard the *Beagle*. Over the years, Darwin and Goose Green had become famous not only for the battle but for bird watching, fishing, walking, boating, and even golfing.

The further they walked, the more Kevin realised how little there was to see. The battlefield ahead was just a typical green field like the ones back in Scotland. Miles and miles of grassy fields, sea, and rivers to the side. Apart from a few pieces of cloth from ex-Argentine blankets and empty British anti-tank missile cases, there was little evidence a battle had ever taken place here. Even the minefield signs that he had seen on the internet were gone as all the mines had been cleared a few years earlier. All that remained of the war were a few memorials scattered across the landscape— plaques and engraved stones surrounded by poppy sticks and cards, marking the spot where a loved one had fallen.

Most of the memorials, the guide informed him, were past Darwin, the settlement where they were staying for the night. There was the memorial where Lieutenant Colonel H Jones had fallen, up the infamous gorse gully. A little further on, in the same area, the 2 PARA Memorial rested at the top of the ridge and provided a great view of Goose Green in the distance, listing the names of the British who had given their lives.

Kevin learnt that his father's battalion had been the first to land at San Carlos. By the time the battle got underway, they had already walked many miles, a very long, tiring trek carrying heavy loads on their backs through marshy, soggy land. They had been hungry and exhausted. Many of them, as Frank had correctly told him, were already suffering from the symptoms of trench foot, but most refused to admit to it in case they were sent back to San Carlos. When Kevin queried why this was, he was told this battle was something they had been looking forward to, the culmination of months of waiting and travelling. On top of that, many British soldiers and marines had already died in ships by this point and now at last, they were in the position to address this.

Kevin tried to picture his father, proudly representing his country, raring to go forward into battle. Youthful, skilled, and cocky, answering the call of duty, this was a job he had been trained to do. He listened intently as the guide told him how many things had gone wrong. Terrible weather, faulty equipment, lack of sleep. It certainly wasn't the one-sided quick victory reported back home. Vital supplies had been lost in the sinking of the SS *Atlantic Conveyor.* The HMS *Arrow* was supposed to be supporting 2 PARA into battle, but the ship's guns jammed at a critical moment. There was poor artillery and mortar support. The list of cock-ups was endless, but most famously of all, the BBC had decided to announce on the world service radio station that 2 PARA were about to attack Darwin and Goose Green. Luckily, no damage was actually done.

From time to time, as he listened to the guide with interest, Kevin looked behind to check that Frank was okay, but after a while, as he engrossed himself further in the stories of his father's battle, he forgot to check.

Chapter 24

As Frank set off behind Kevin and the guide, it didn't bother him that the pace was too fast and the distance between them quickly began to widen. He wanted to be alone, to take his time, and besides, he distrusted the guide who was only there because of veterans like him. Other people had made the sacrifices so that guides like him could earn money showing tourists around old battlegrounds like this one. Perhaps the guide had a better knowledge of the history of the battle than he had, but he hadn't been in the battle itself. He could never understand the sights, the sounds, the smells of warfare. He would never experience the sensations of large explosive impacts, the fizzing sounds of tiny shrapnel and bullets flying past one's head.

He found it difficult to take in the vast fields ahead of him. It seemed so peaceful that trying to reconcile the acres of natural farmland with a vicious battle that had claimed so many lives was difficult. For decades he had been suffering because of the events that took place here. He had returned home alive, but this war had taken over his life.

The further they walked, the more confused he became. The landscape was different from what he had imagined. It was just a flat field, so perhaps the rocks and mounds were further up? He did remember the feel of the ground, sodden and covered with brackish water, the round tussocks of grass known as "babies heads," nicknamed because of the damage they did to the soldiers' legs, twisting ankles and knees as they tried to advance in the dark. He remembered setting off that night too. The battle was already underway, and he could see the fireworks and hear the noise of fighting in the distance.

What did surprise him was another emotion that creeped up on him as he walked. Hate and an angry sense of injustice that so many people had died needlessly on these grounds. Anger for the slaughter of his comrades, hatred for the enemy. Before the war began, the Argentineans had been merely a faceless enemy. They were soldiers just like him. They had come here to do a job, nothing more. It was the politicians who were the real enemy. But as lives were lost, that perception began to change.

There were lives to avenge. Many lives had already been lost in the water back in San Carlos, sunk in their ships. Any feelings of reconciliation or forgiveness were quickly forgotten. That night, he had set off with another stretcher bearer into the darkness, armed with loads of ammo, and the enemy had blatantly fired at him despite strict Geneva convention rules about such actions. Later, it was discovered that the Argentineans had been trying to drop napalm on the British Forces. Buildings and even dead bodies were booby trapped. One incident had enraged him more than any other—a white flag had been waved outside a schoolhouse and three members of 12 Platoon had gone up to accept the surrender and negotiate only to be shot dead as they approached.

Just thinking about these incidents now, the strong emotion of hate consumed him. His body began to shiver, and he had to stop and rest. He sat down on the grass.

As his open hands touched the wet grass, he had a sudden flashback. It was not a nightmare this time but a memory.

"Ker chunk, ker chunk," he could hear.

As his eyes grew accustomed to the darkness, he realised he was lying face down on the wet ground. He was soaked to the skin, and his legs were bruised by the rocky ground he had been crawling over. His hands were numb with cold, and the muscles on his neck and shoulders were clenched like a vice.

Straight away, he looked for his rock. He knew he was on Darwin Ridge somewhere. Was this the bottom? That's when he heard someone next to him whispering. He had never heard a voice so scared in his life before.

"It's going to be a fucking massacre," the terrified voice said from nearby.

Frank could see the mist from the mouth that had uttered the words. Turning to his right, he could make out a long line of soldiers all lying in the same position he was. All still. All waiting. Waiting.

His eyes were shut now. Was he remembering the start of the battle? Why now? Was being here on the walk today to Darwin really all it took for the memory to be jogged and prodded? He could feel the hairs rising on his arms and the sweat that came from the adrenaline and raw fear.

Terrified, he slowly looked up ahead of him. In the far distance, he could see a darker shadow, a mound. It slightly resembled a mountain, but it was too far away for him to be sure. He tried to focus, soon thinking he could make out a series of hollows, rocky ledges, undulations, outcrops.

He gulped as he realised where he was. He was at the bottom of the ridge, waiting for the order to attack. Up there somewhere in the distance, the enemy were waiting for them. Waiting to kill them. Up there was slaughter and death, and everyone could feel it.

"Fucking hell, we are all going to die," he heard another terrified soldier whisper.

These were the same lads who had laughed and joked on the journey over, looking forward to a good fight, bragging and overconfident young lads now reduced to whimpering, scared kids. To his left, out of the corner of his eye, he thought he saw little pinpricks of white and red flashing lights in the far distance.

Then his thoughts were quickly disturbed by the loud, booming voice of the commanding officer. "Fix bayonets, lads."

He could hear that special sound now, a loud series of scrapes as the blades were pulled from their scabbards and the double but slow "Ker chunkkk" as they were fixed into position.

"Ker chunk, ker chunk," echoed all around him.

"No prisoners, lads. No prisoners," came the final order.

"Ker chunk, ker chunk."

Frank opened his eyes. The flashback was over, but the sounds still echoed inside his head, reverberating.

"Ker chunk, ker chunk."

Coming around, he saw Kevin and the guide gathered around him, talking to him, looking concerned.

"Frank, are you okay? Talk to me, Frank," Kevin shouted to him over the wind.

Frank tried to say something but gasped instead. "I remember," he eventually managed to blurt out. "I remember..."

"What, Frank? What do you remember?"

"The bastards...they—" His eyes were full of tears, but he was fighting to hold them back. The hatred overwhelmed him, sapping his strength.

"What, Frank? What do you remember?" Kevin shouted a little louder, trying to get his attention.

As Frank looked around, he was confused. They were much further on than he had realised. He was not sure how long they had been walking now. He would have suggested ten minutes, but the scene around him had changed so much. He must have forgotten or misjudged how far he had been walking. All the stress of being here, the memories, the flashbacks, must have played a part. The land was no longer flat but full of hills, mounds of gorse and bracken. To his left, he could see a little collection of houses, sheep, and distant figures of people walking around.

Confused, he managed to ask Kevin, "Kev, where the fuck are we?"

"This is Darwin, Frank. Darwin Ridge."

He thought Kevin was playing a joke, so he immediately turned to the guide, but he made no gesture to correct him.

"You okay, Frank? The lodge is just over there. We can stop and rest for the day."

"No, Kevin, stop fucking about. Where's Darwin? I don't see it," Frank cursed. They couldn't be near Darwin yet. Last time, the land had been covered in smoke, darkness, but he remembered the granite structures further up the hill. And that wasn't anywhere to be seen.

"This isn't D-Darwin, you arsehole. There are n-no rocks here," Frank stuttered.

"What do you mean, Frank?"

"I mean Darwin Ridge...it's not here. What's the fucking matter with you, Kevin?"

It was the guide who intervened, perhaps afraid Frank was losing his temper. "You must be confused, Frank. I've been doing these tours for over ten years. That's Darwin Ridge right there...over there. See that stone on the ridge? That's where Jones was killed and got his Victoria Cross." He pointed straight ahead.

That was the moment Frank ran off. His tired legs were forced to find the energy needed, adrenaline taking over as he ran towards the ridge. This time it was Kevin who was trying to keep up, running after him.

This couldn't be Darwin Ridge. He had expected it to be much bigger, steeper. He had also expected it to be rockier. There was no mountain or rocky, jagged edges, rather it was more of a small fold, a bump. This hill was covered in grass, circles of yellow and green gorse bushes. In his mind, it was just mud and earth and rocks, but this hill was just grass. Even the angle of the hill seemed wrong. He'd thought it was much steeper. And where were the rocks?

"It's just over there," Frank stuttered, pointing to the hill. It didn't matter that Kevin was too far behind to hear. He was talking to himself. He knew he had to find his rock. The rock in the dreams, that would prove it.

Find the rock. Find the rock.

Deciding it had to be on the other side of the hill, he passed the memorial for Lt. Colonel Jones but did not stop to read it. Everywhere now was gorse. Big lumps of grass, yellow and gorse bushes. He remembered this place, but it was not the place from his dreams. This was not where he had been ambushed, where the phosphorous grenade had exploded further up, where he had witnessed the enemy body rolling down before coming to rest beside him.

The longer he stood on the small fold trying to make sense of everything, the more upset he became. His eyes twitched, and he was unable to stand still, fidgeting and scratching his head, not willing to accept what his eyesight was witnessing, searching manically for the distinctive white rock from his dreams.

Find the rock. Find the rock.

He knew exactly what the rock looked like. He just needed to find it. It was, he reminded himself as he sprinted across the half-mile-long width of the ridge, two feet high, barely high enough for his long, thin frame to hide behind. He could picture the coarse texture, the white-grey stone with its uneven, steeply inclined formation. He could picture the sharp, jagged edges and the odd different-coloured moss growing on its surface. He could even still smell it, the phosphorous and smell of burning flesh not something a normal human could ever forget. Most of all, it was the distinctive shape he could still picture, like two rocks had been clumsily glued together to resemble a deformed rectangle.

But it was nowhere to be seen. The rock was not there.

A great sense of panic washed over him, but he sat down on the hill and tried to think his dilemma through logically. He figured he must have missed it, that perhaps he had not searched each area thoroughly enough. He tried to remember that at the time of the ambush, he was being bombarded by artillery from the enemy and it was also dark.

He ran back and started retracing his steps as Kevin tried to stop him. Going over the same steps again and again, he obsessively ran around in circles, rechecking everything one more time just to be sure.

Had it been taken away because some sheep hurt itself on it or because it threatened to break some farm machine? Maybe it was even simpler than that. Perhaps it all looked so different when you were being ambushed in the darkness of night. They called it "the fog of war." Perhaps when you were freezing, tired and continually under fire, as he had been that day, everything you saw seemed exaggerated. Maybe it was actually a smaller rock than he imagined. Or maybe the rock had been moved or destroyed. Maybe some tourists had stolen it for a souvenir. But it couldn't have simply disintegrated with years of wind and rain, worn out by time.

Kevin had now finally managed to catch up with him. A few yards behind him, the guide was screaming into his mobile, trying to call for medical help. His legs finally buckled, and he collapsed onto the grass, a broken man. His eyes were staring up at the sky, failing to focus.

"I don't understand," Frank finally managed to gasp as Kevin stood over him, out of breath.

"What is it, Frank? What is it?" Kevin shouted desperately, gasping for air.

"The rock...it's not here!" Frank screamed out. "It's not fucking here!"

It was only when he saw Kevin's puzzled expression that Frank finally realised what was happening. For years, he had been certain his ambush had taken place on Darwin Hill, but now he understood it was all a lie. He had been here in the battle, but it was not here that the nightmares had been about. The nightmares that had tormented him for years had not taken place at Darwin but at Wireless Ridge. His mind had jumbled them up. The battles had been mixed up.

That was the moment he passed out.

Chapter 25

As Kevin left the hospital and walked down the main street of Port Stanley, he felt relieved that everything had not been as bad as he'd first feared. Despite the drama of the last five hours, Frank had not had a heart attack but simply passed out. When he regained consciousness a few minutes later, an air ambulance had been called as a precaution and flown Frank to the King Edward VII Memorial Hospital in Port Stanley. Frank was going to be okay, but he needed to rest. He had been ordered to stay overnight in the hospital and, when released in the morning, to remain in Stanley for the rest of the trip. There were to be no more visits to old battlegrounds, and all the trips in the pipeline for them had now been cancelled.

Despite the relief, it had been frustrating. Up until the moment they reached Darwin, the trip had been going so well. Excited to see Darwin in the distance for the first time, he had been so emotionally engaged in his surroundings, walking and chatting with the guide, that he hadn't noticed Frank becoming very agitated. Rushing over to him, he noticed Frank was disoriented, confused about his whereabouts, refusing to believe they were in Darwin. Frank had then run off in a panic towards the ridge. By the time Kevin finally managed to catch up with him, Frank was in some kind of trance and shouting, "It's not here! It's not here," before eventually collapsing.

At least Port Stanley wasn't the worst place for Frank to be grounded. There were plenty of things here to keep him happy, like memorials, tourist attractions, bars and restaurants. Most importantly of all, Jack, the taxi driver, lived here and would be around to take care of Frank. Already, they were becoming very close friends, relieving Kevin of the burden of constantly looking after Frank.

There was good news waiting for Kevin as he checked into his hotel room. As he opened his laptop, he noticed a Facebook chat message from Dave Townsend waiting for him.

Excitedly, Kevin read the message.

> Hi, Kevin. Hope you are enjoying your trip. You asked for help with retracing your dad's last steps, and I've been asking around. It's possible that your dad wasn't treated at Ajax Bay or on the SS *Uganda*. Apparently, there was an advanced surgical centre at Teal Inlet. I've been told they treated some 223 casualties of various conditions in that short time, which is not often mentioned or in the books. This cut the travel distance and time to Ajax, saving a lot of lives.
>
> I was also wondering whether you have thought about asking around about your dad's dog tags. All of 2 PARA wore two identical dog tags around their neck—one to identify the body and the other to remain with the corpse in case battle conditions prevented the body from being recovered. They were stainless steel circle badges attached to a knotted

leather brown string. Attached to them would have been two morphine syrettes.

Anyway, just in case, I did a bit of digging and found out your dad's dog tags would have probably been inscribed as:

OPOS (Not sure of your dad's blood type, so this is a guess.)

24445513 (His service number, this I have checked.)

TURNER (Surname)

BR (Initials, Baz Robert)

CE (Church of England, religious preference.)

Hope that helps.

Best Wishes,

Dave

As Kevin digested the information, he felt excited. It was another clue, a possible lead that might help him find his father's last location. Whatever had happened to his dad all those years ago, it was a fact that his dog tags did exist. As he pondered on his next move, he realised the new information had come at a perfect time. With Frank grounded in Port Stanley, there would be no more disruption. He could continue investigating his father's last footsteps in his own good time, no longer needing to constantly look behind his shoulder in fear of what Frank was up to.

Excited, he began to think of the options available. Perhaps he could hire a car and go back to Goose Green, see the memorials he had been unable to see this morning. There was Ajax Bay in San Carlos to visit too. There was a museum there that might be able to help. There also had to be some government building on these islands where he could enquire about where war memorabilia was stored.

Of course, he knew it was a shot in the dark. A long time had passed, and the chances of finding his father's dog tags were miniscule. These islands were twelve thousand square kilometres big, and what if they were lost at sea or in another country?

But it didn't matter—this was the first time he had something positive to go on. The bits of the puzzle were now starting to fit into place. Excited, Kevin picked up his mobile and made a call.

Chapter 26

It was nearly ten o'clock in the evening, ten hours since Frank had first arrived at the hospital. The drugs were working well, and he felt relaxed. The doctors had told him that if everything went okay, he would be allowed to leave in the morning.

So far, his hospital stay hadn't been too unpleasant. He had his own room, and the beds were bigger and more comfortable than back home in Dundee. Clean, fresh sea air wafted through the open window, bringing with it the noise of happy people wandering around nearby. The hospital food was an improvement too—tea and homemade cake mid-afternoon.

He had so many visitors that he hadn't even had time to dwell on earlier events. Jack had been to visit him, arriving with a huge bouquet of flowers and a card containing the best wishes from all the staff in the Victory Bar. There had also been a brief visit from Kevin. But it was the unexpected visit from Fiona that had really made his day. As soon as she walked in, Frank's mood immediately lifted. He found it difficult not to stare at her with the refreshingly normal jeans and T-shirt. There was something so innocent about her that made her approachable. There were no politics or rules with this woman. Unlike before in his life, no games needed to be played and no rules needed to be followed. He felt he could be himself.

Unfortunately, visiting hours were not long, but the disappointment he'd felt when she left a few hours earlier was cancelled out by the present she had given him—a brand-new mobile phone. Normally, he would have politely declined such a gift had it been given by anyone else. Not only was he a genuine technophobe but he had always intensely disliked mobiles. They were a necessary evil, an intrusion of privacy, and he found them traumatising, the alarms reminding him of the war.

He had never expected to admit a mobile phone could serve a purpose, but after a few lessons from Fiona, he couldn't live without it. She had taught him how to make the phone silent, so it was never annoying, and, over the last hour, they had been furiously exchanging text messages. Receiving photos of Fiona had made his mouth water and put a smile back on his face.

Now, as night fell, there was a scary silence. Fiona had gone to bed and stopped sending messages. It became harder to ignore the thoughts of earlier. Obviously, he'd had some kind of flashback, just like in the pub garden and on the bus back home. He remembered clearly arriving at Camilla Creek and recalled the hate that had consumed him as he walked across the field. He remembered too the flashback of lying in the dark and that unpleasant sound of attaching bayonets as they waited for the order to attack.

He knew what had happened but struggled to accept it. His brain had deceived him. He hadn't found the rock at Darwin because there were no rocks there. The rock was not at Darwin but at Wireless Ridge, and suddenly he had no conception of what was real and what was made up. The doctors had ordered him to rest, that he take no more trips and must remain in Port Stanley. Anything that involved revisiting the past and traumatising him was to cease. They reasoned that there was a big connection between trauma and memory loss. "Psychogenic Amnesia," the doctors had said, that his memory loss was related to memories so stressful or traumatic that the mind resorts to amnesia in order to cope.

The trouble was that he wasn't ready to stop. He had spent nearly his whole life living under the shadow of this war, survivor's guilt, nightmares and the loss of memory. And now, the truth about the war was finally within his grasp? How could he stop when he was so close?

His memory was definitely returning. Just in the last month alone, he had learnt so much more about Baz, the necklace, the location of the rock. Today he had recalled the order to fix bayonets, the hatred for the enemy.

Whatever the doctors advised, he knew he couldn't stop now. There were only seven days left, and he knew he would never be on these islands again. He was too old to come back here and would never be able to afford the trip alone. It had to be done now.

Besides what was real and what wasn't? How bad could finding out the truth be? He had lived with not remembering how he had been shot for decades and now had come so far that there was nothing to lose. The truth was finally within his grasp.

With a clear sense of purpose and determination, he got out of bed and walked to the window. Looking out, he saw the sun still setting, the sky a beautiful mix of red and orange colours. As the sun slowly descended into the horizon and darkness arrived, something niggled at him. He couldn't put his finger on what it was, but something seemed familiar. He remembered he had felt this way last night too, from the hotel window down the road. But he was adamant had never been here before, not in Port Stanley.

Was it the view, the sea air, the wind? Maybe it was because it looked so innocent and small, like a little village in Scotland, and it reminded him of home?

Eventually he closed the window, shut the curtains, and got back into bed. Exhausted, sleep came quickly and so did the dream.

It was total darkness, so he had no idea where he was, but the smell was terrible. A smell of grease coupled with burnt flesh and seaweed. As he attempted to get up and move around to orientate himself, he discovered he was lying flat on his back, tied down, his waist, arms, and legs restrained by some kind of belt. He wondered if he was just imagining it—perhaps he was paralysed as the only movement he could make was to move his head slightly horizontally to his right.

Hearing muffled sounds, he realised he was not alone. Straining his ears for more clues, he could make out the sound of heavy breathing interrupted by sniffles and grunts. People were quietly groaning in pain. Sensing his body was gently moving up and down, he realised he must be in a ship of some kind. He could feel that his head was on some kind of head rest and cotton sheets were covering him up. Then he looked to his immediate right and saw a man sitting up in his bed, covered in bandages except for holes where the eyes stared at him. Around his neck was a necklace, glistening in the moonlight. Thinking it might be Baz's necklace, he calmly reached out for it, hoping to examine it closer.

That was when the bandaged man started to whisper to him, "Find the rock, find the rock."

The bandaged head, then exploded and covered Frank in a red mist.

When Frank awoke, there was no panic or screaming. Perhaps it was the medication he was on, but apart from being soaked with sweat, he felt no need to press the emergency button to call a nurse for help. He felt empowered and triumphant. The nightmares didn't scare him anymore. Instead, he felt a sense of revelation. For the first time ever, he felt he was finally winning. Another puzzle piece had emerged.

He had never been to Port Stanley. He had never been to Ajax Bay either. After being shot at Wireless Ridge, he had been sent to the SS *Uganda*, the British hospital ship. That was the ship where his dream had just taken place.

He was getting closer to the truth now. He had to keep going.

REALITY

Chapter 27

As Frank looked out of his tiny plane window, he couldn't believe how lucky he was. They called them FIGAS planes, property of the Falkland Islands, a group of Britten-Norman BN-2B Islander ten-seater aircraft that made getting around the islands a lot easier. It was thrilling to be in such a small plane, watching the beauty of the islands from high above. He had expected to be scared of heights, but the views were so astonishing, they took his breath away.

One of the eight passengers on this plane, seated next to him was Jack. Together they were finally on their way to San Carlos. Jack had become a true friend over the last few days. What had started off as a short taxi ride had developed into a meaningful friendship. Jack had told him that he had never forgotten the sacrifices of the British in freeing them and, ever grateful, would do anything to make veterans feel welcome. Now that Frank had been in the hospital, it had become Jack's mission to ensure he got everything he needed and was treated like royalty.

Accordingly, four days earlier when he was let out of the hospital, Jack had insisted he move out of the hotel and into his house in the capital. Jack had personally picked him up and driven him to his house where, for the last few days, he and his wife had spoilt him with delicious food and "Smoko," the island's tradition of cakes and coffee.

Not that Jack had to try hard to make him feel at home! Fiona was his next-door neighbour and only too happy to pop in and keep Frank company. They had spent the last few days getting to know each other better, talking a lot. He had managed to tell Fiona about his lack of memory and the trauma he had been forever running away from.

Yesterday, Jack and Fiona had taken him to see the 1982 Liberation Memorial. Frank had been very emotional to learn it was constructed to commemorate all the British Forces and supporting units that served in the war. Funds were raised entirely from Falkland Islanders. It was an obelisk, on the front of which was the coat of arms of the Falkland Islands surrounded by a laurel wreath above the words, "In Memory of Those Who Liberated Us" and the date the war ended, "14 June 1982." On the back and sides of the Memorial were lists of the British Army regiments, RAF squadrons, Royal Navy vessels and the Royal Marine formations and units that took part in the conflict and the names of the 255 British military personnel who died during the war.

Seeing the memorial had only strengthened his determination to use the last week as constructively as possible. He confided to Fiona that he couldn't help but feel he was wasting valuable time by obeying doctor's orders and staying put in Stanley. He needed to address his survivor's guilt, to get the pieces of his missing memory back.

That was when Fiona had suggested a visit to San Carlos. Not only was this where the British had landed but it also had a cemetery where Frank could pay his respects. Blue Beach Military Cemetery, as it was known, only held 13 of the 255 casualties, but it was also a memorial for all those who had died in the sea. What better place to address his survivor's guilt, Fiona had opined.

After Fiona discussed the idea with Jack, Jack had sprung into action like a demon possessed. Strings were pulled, phone calls made, and favours used up. Frank was amused to discover that Jack knew so many people by first name. One of his friends was a pilot with FIGAS, and another friend in San Carlos was a doctor. Jack pleaded with the hospital to allow the trip, arguing that San Carlos was not actually a battleground in the same way as Goose Green or others. Jack was given the all-clear as long as he was with Frank at all times and that Frank took his prescribed medicine. The only downside to the trip today was that Fiona had to work and would be unable to join them. However, they had arranged to meet after he returned later in the day.

As they landed on the field at Port San Carlos, Frank was surprised that he remembered so much. They got in a car, Frank's face lighting up as Jack pointed out the Sussex Mountains in the background where 2 PARA had trekked up after landing. The place was just as he had expected and remembered, a quiet, empty place, unspoiled. Apart from the presence of the British war cemetery and a small war museum, there really was nothing else there. Just like Goose Green, this place could have easily passed for some farmland in the middle of Scotland.

"Do those mountains look familiar, Frank?"

"It's difficult to be sure, Jack. It's so long ago," Frank had replied, too embarrassed to admit he had always felt a bit ashamed that he had not "yomped" up the mountains like everyone else but been given a lift in a helicopter.

With Jack's phone GPS, they managed to trace the exact location in Bomb Alley where the MV *Norland* had been anchored. Jack proudly pointed out the areas where all the different regiments had landed and showed Frank the buoy that marked the spot where HMS *Antelope* had been sunk.

Frank didn't really remember much of the views, only what it was like to be stuck on a ship, helpless to prevent the enemy jets as they swooped down to drop their missiles on the British fleet. He had forgotten until now the terrible conditions on his ship that had made him so desperate to get off. The fear of being on heightened alert, of waiting to be bombed.

"What is it, Frank? You okay?"

"It's just being back here. I remember," he said sadly.

"What do you remember?"

"A word that sent shivers down my spine every time I heard it." Frank swallowed and closed his eyes.

"What word was that?" asked Jack.

Frank took a deep breath and said, "Exocet."

"Oh, I see." Jack looked like he knew what he was talking about.

"Yeah, the missile they dropped from the Argie jets. What made them so terrifying was they avoided air defences by flying in low, which meant nobody saw them coming until it was too late. We were just sitting ducks. Our ships' defences were simply not adequately equipped to deal with the threat. And I was stuck on some sea ferry. I remember just begging the CO to let me go onshore."

Jack nodded, not willing to interrupt.

"God, it was really tense, like sitting on the edge of your seat twenty-four hours a day. There were constant false alarms and stuff. As each wave came in, there would be a panicky 'Take cover! Take cover!' over the ship radio. We were all on the top decks, and I would throw myself under a table. No protection at all! I felt very helpless and vulnerable on the boat. There really was nowhere to run or hide as the sea was freezing. There was nothing you could do but pray—your life was in the hands of fate. I was lucky though, Jack. I eventually got moved ashore, but even then, I still had to watch some ships getting sunk. Do you know what pissed me off most, Jack?"

"Tell me, Frank."

"So many ships were hit but didn't sink. People only remember those that sunk, but so many were hit and didn't." Frank was now shaking in anger.

"Yeah, I heard about that. The fuses in the bomb didn't go off, right?"

"Yeah, because of the low altitude of the aerial attacks. Apparently, the fuses didn't have time to arm the bombs. But, you know..." His voice was starting to rise again now. "This was disclosed by some journalist reporting on the war. Disgraceful." It was the same angry feeling he'd had at Darwin, but determined not to let Jack down and spoil the day, he tried to gather himself.

They started walking again, and Frank began to feel better. However, he was unprepared for the overwhelming sadness that hit him as they approached the nearby Blue Beach Military Cemetery. In this small plot of land lay the remains of fourteen of the British casualties killed in the war. Given the small number of actual graves, this was more of a memorial monument than a cemetery. Even from a distance, you could tell it was a special place, beautifully preserved and treated with reverence. The area was enclosed by a metre-high stone wall with a small entrance open to the beach in the style of sheep corrals that used to be typical landmarks in the Falklands. Opposite the entrance, the wall was tapered higher with seven slate panels on which the names of soldiers were inscribed. As he approached, the wind began to really blow and the icy wind stung his ears.

Frank at once noticed the large memorial plaques at the rear of the circular wall. As he reached the gate, he felt short of breath. Here lay the remains of people he had once admired, once aspired to be with. These were soldiers, many of whom he had fought alongside in the Battle of Goose Green. That day, promoted to assist the platoon because of a lack of available paratroopers, he had fought in the same battle with these brave men—some names he recognised, some he had even helped stretcher safely back to the medics.

Pausing for breath, he leaned against the cemetery wall. Time had passed so quickly that Frank had forgotten many of the people who died in the Falklands War weren't killed on the battlefields but were the people who had never even made it ashore. They were on the ships when they died. It wasn't just the HMS *Sheffield* or the *Atlantic Conveyor* that had been sunk out in the seas. Two frigates, HMS *Ardent* and HMS *Antelope*, as well as the destroyer HMS *Coventry* had been lost as well. Out there in the cold, unfriendly sea was the resting place of one hundred and seventy-four British people, buried at sea, lost with their aircraft or ships.

He opened the gate and beckoned Jack to join him. Together they walked very slowly around, reading the names inscribed on the panels. When they got to the main panel inscription, Frank rested his right arm on Jack's shoulder for support as his croaky voice read out the inscription, oblivious to the small crowd of others walking around.

IN HONOUR OF

THE SOUTH ATLANTIC TASK FORCE
AND TO THE ABIDING MEMORY OF
THE SAILORS SOLDIERS AND AIRMEN
WHO GAVE THEIR LIVES AND WHO
HAVE NO GRAVE BUT THE SEA
HERE BESIDE THE
GRAVES OF THEIR COMRADES THIS
MEMORIAL RECORDS THEIR NAMES

He knelt down on the grass and thought of those who had lost their lives, remembering their sacrifice. He thought of his mother, of the heavy price she had also paid for his war. Kevin too—his life had been profoundly changed by events here and this trip to the Falklands was his journey too.

But mostly, as he stood in this small cemetery barely sheltered from the strong winds, he thought of his friend, Baz Turner. Frank had never been religious before, but standing here, he wanted nothing more than to tell Baz he had tried to keep his promise. He wanted to tell Baz he had taken care of Kevin, his son, given him a loving home despite the difficult circumstances. Kevin had neither been forgotten nor given up for adoption. And the proof was here today. Kevin was not with him, but he was on these islands, going on small trips alone, proudly treading where his father's footsteps had once trodden. Baz's death had not been in vain because his legacy lived on in his son.

After all the years of denial, Frank finally understood what remembrance meant to him. Before today, it had just been words—words of compassion, words of comfort, words of commiseration, words of regret. But now they were words that had never made more sense. Being here today was a reminder that these soldiers never had the opportunity to grow old, to have kids or be grandparents. They never had to deal with bills, mortgages, marriage or work. These people had never been able to just walk into a pub like Frank did everyday back in Scotland.

Baz's sacrifice had been the ultimate one, and now Frank finally understood, finally got it. As he bent down on his knees, he spoke out loud, boldly and unafraid,

"They shall grow not old,

as we that are left grow old:

Age shall not weary them,

nor the years condemn.

At the going down of the sun

and in the morning,

we will remember them,

we will remember them."

It took a long time before Frank was composed and ready enough to stand up and leave the cemetery. Jack asked if he wanted to go to Ajax Bay, but the visit to the cemetery had shaken Frank up and he was clearly not up to it. He felt tired.

"No worries, mate," Jack whispered. "There is nothing there anyway, mate...just an empty building."

Reaching into his pocket, Frank took some pills and a sip of his prized half bottle of scotch.

"Let's get out of here," Frank muttered. "Let's go back to the Victory."

Chapter 28

As Kevin lay on the hotel bed watching the local news, he reflected on the frustration of the last couple of days. He now had a money problem. Hiring a lawyer to try to get the government to cough up the truth had cost him more than he had expected and there had been a few problems with his bank cards. Money was hopefully soon forthcoming, but trying to sort out his finances from the other side of the world was going to take time. In the meantime, as most services had been cancelled because of a lack of tourists, there were no cars to hire, no guides to book, and no flights available. He had been marooned in Port Stanley for three days now, stranded like a dead whale.

Despite the setbacks, he had tried to be positive and spent the last couple of days visiting Port Stanley's churches and memorials, the Dockyard Museum, the seafront, Victory Green and the Governor's house. However, he had quickly grown tired of the quaint little seaside town and felt restless, acutely aware that time was slowly ticking away. There were now only four days until the flight home and time for retracing his father's footsteps was running out fast.

What made his dilemma worse was that, while he was stuck in Port Stanley, Frank was busy flying around the islands, visiting the very places Kevin himself wanted to visit. He had heard that today Frank visited San Carlos, not far from Ajax Bay, one of the last possible sightings of his dad. As much as he tried to understand, he seethed with jealousy, feeling abandoned and forgotten. He felt Frank was strutting around like a proud peacock, enjoying his newfound celebrity status. The local population seemed to worship anyone who had help liberate them, but nobody seemed to care that Kevin's dad had been a liberator too. To further rub salt in his wounds, Frank had switched off his phone and was not returning his calls.

Bored and frustrated, Kevin spent a lot of his spare time online in his hotel room, trying to enquire about his father's dog tags. Trouble was that it was a difficult task— the information simply wasn't available. So much time had passed, and records had been misplaced or lost. Even trying to approach the subject with veterans online had revealed another problem. So many people had gone to war, different people in different places, each with specific and contra- dictory memories. Even those who did remember some- thing understandably didn't feel comfortable regurgitating possible theories and addressing rumours, mostly unsub- stantiated.

Luckily for Kevin, a little progress had been made with Dave Townsend, the same veteran who had first sent him the information about his father's dog tags. It seemed ironic that he had probably learnt more today about his father's last remaining whereabouts than from nearly forty years of knowing Frank. With Dave, there were no family complica- tions involved, no stubborn denials or lost memories. Only a sadness that he was learning things he should have been told many years ago.

Chatting with Dave had uncovered another theory for his father's disappearance in 1982—the knock-on effect of the events of the eighth of June. On that day, enemy Skyhawk jets had swooped down and hit RFA *Sir Galahad* and RFA *Sir Tristram*, leading to the biggest single loss suffered by the British during the conflict. Fifty-six people were killed and one hundred and fifty were wounded.

Dave had explained that the reason the tragedy might have affected his father was because most of the injured from the tragedy were first taken to Ajax Bay, the very place his father had been recuperating. To make space for the huge numbers of injured, it was almost certain that, because his shrapnel injuries were lower medical priority, Kevin's father was moved elsewhere. Where he was moved to, however, Dave could only speculate. If Baz still needed further treatment, he could have been flown to HMS *Intrepid* or HMS *Fearless*, troopships with big flight decks and full medical teams. Another possibility was, as they had discussed before, that he had ended up on the SS *Uganda*, the hospital ship. However, Dave believed the most likely scenario was that Baz had recovered well from his wounds by the time the *Galahad* was hit and was thus ordered to rejoin his battalion at Fitzroy.

This was when Kevin became confused. "But Fitzroy was the very same place the tragedy had taken place. Why would they meet up there?" he had typed impatiently.

Dave explained that 2 PARA were already there. At the time, military plans were already focusing on the main goal of surrounding and recapturing the areas around Port Stanley. Fitzroy had been chosen because of its close proximity to Stanley and its easy accessibility by sea. Five thousand new troops were arriving to strengthen the task force.

"So," typed Kevin, "2 PARA were there when the tragedy happened?"

"Yes, 2 PARA witnessed the whole tragedy as it unfolded. Some others and I, we were fishing at the time when we heard the planes coming in to attack. We watched the whole thing unfold, unable to do anything until the life rafts arrived. If you look on YouTube, it's 2 PARA pulling in the ropes of the boats and helping administer first aid."

Kevin was shocked to hear this. Until now, he had no idea that 2 PARA were at Fitzroy. Why should he? Whenever it was mentioned, it was always the Welsh guards they spoke about. He decided to ask the veteran the six-million-dollar question. "But, if my dad was sent to Fitzroy, why did he never make it?"

"I guess because the *Galahad* tragedy changed everything. Helicopters were already scarce and, with so many injured and killed, all the available helicopters that might have escorted your dad back were instead used to move the wounded. He was probably stranded in Ajax Bay."

"He could have taken a ship, surely?" Kevin typed.

The veteran replied that he doubted that because the geography of the islands presented too many problems. Fitzroy was only forty-five miles south of Stanley, sixty miles east across land from San Carlos. But by ship, it was a very long diversion. You were forced to sail south down the Falkland sound, east to Sea Lion Island and then north again. The veteran guessed such a journey was at least four hundred miles and would take at least three days. Besides, the veteran argued, if Baz had taken a ship, why was he reported as MIA? If the ship had sunk, why were there no records of it?

Dave reminded him that this was all speculation, but it also seemed to make sense, especially when the veteran then explained the concept of "fog of war." Even something so simple as getting from A to B with hindsight became complicated. The *Galahad* tragedy was a classic example—an event caused by endless delays and bickering in getting the troops off the ship. There was confusion about directions, locations, and who was in command. People became separated, orders become confused and subject to revision due to poor communication. This all resulted in a continuing uncertainty, a perceptual "fog."

As Kevin took all this information in, he remembered the theories Frank had shared with him a few months ago in the pub back home in Tayport. "Is it possible he deserted, got lost, or there was friendly fire or something?" he typed.

"Not possible at all. If any of those things had happened, he would not have been reported as missing in action."

"But surely it's possible he deserted, isn't it?"

"Of course, it's possible, but it was common knowledge that your dad was just not the type. Your dad was one of the very best paratroopers. He was loyal, brave and popular. If I had to guess, it's possible that he went off by foot from Ajax Bay and got lost. You've seen how the islands are, right?"

There was a long pause in the typing as Kevin tried to explore every possibility while the veteran was online. "What about a cover-up?" he eventually typed.

"I don't know. Why? What was there to hide?" the veteran typed, trying to be helpful. "By the way, remember that 2 PARA were only in Fitzroy another thirty-six hours before we were dispatched."

"Thirty-six hours?" Kevin's mood fell. This was getting complicated now.

"Roughly, yeah. After the tragedy at Fitzroy, there was an increased determination to get the job done. That's why, because of the tragedy at Fitzroy, 2 PARA were ordered to head towards Stanley and help."

Kevin sighed. Obviously, his father never made it to Fitzroy in time. He was going to ask the veteran about the SAS theory of Frank's, but now he wanted some time to go over what he had learned. Besides, with no body, everything was just speculation. Whatever your theory was, the areas of land and sea involved where he might have been were too large to pinpoint with any hope of accuracy. Instead, Kevin thanked the veteran for his help and lay down on his bed.

Curious, he closed his Facebook page and opened YouTube, typing in *Galahad* in the search field. He then watched BBC film footage of the tragedy. It was a film he had watched many times before, but now he watched it with a new perspective, knowing it was actually 2 PARA, his father's battalion, pulling in the orange life rafts of injured survivors arriving ashore. Watching the chaos unfold, he felt how awful it must have been to witness all that tragedy as it unfolded from the beach.

And where was Frank? Had he witnessed the tragedy too?

He noticed Dave Townsend was still online. "More questions, is that okay?" he typed.

"Go ahead, mate."

"Do you know Frank Drysdale?"

"Rings a bell. Not sure. What did he do? Was he in 2 PARA?"

"Sort of. He was attached to 2 PARA. Defence corps or something?"

There was a long silence.

"Lanky Frank? He got shot, didn't he?"

"Yeah! That's him!"

"I remember him vaguely. Why you asking?"

"He's my adopted dad."

"WTF? Your adopted dad? I didn't know that."

Kevin explained how after Baz never came home, his mother had died and Frank had adopted him after the war. "Frank never told me anything. He hid his scars from me for decades," he typed. "I only found out by accident a few months ago."

"I didn't know him personally, but let me ask someone. I'll get back to you."

"Okay."

Kevin's concentration was broken by the sound of a ping from his laptop, a notification. His eyes darted to the screen, expecting some message from his family back home asking him how he was. But it was a message from someone he hadn't spoken to in over twenty-seven years. Pat, Frank's ex-wife. A few weeks ago, he had seen her name popping up on Facebook as someone he might know and sent a greeting. He hadn't really expected her to reply.

"Wow! My goodness, Kevin, it's been years. How are you?"

"Hi, Pat! Yup, it's me. Been a while. Can we FaceTime?"

They exchanged numbers and suddenly Pat appeared on his phone. It was strange to see her again—a face from the past. The years had been kind. Only her hair seemed to be different, greyer and shorter, but she still had that unmistakable look and smile.

"Wow, Kevin," she shrieked with joy. "Last time I saw you, you were just a sweet little boy!"

"Yeah," Kevin said shyly.

"How old are you these days?"

"Forty next year."

"Oh dear, well, if it's any consolation, it's not long until I reach the mighty sixty. Anyway, last time I heard you were working in the games business or something?"

"Yeah, that's right, but guess where I am now?"

"No idea."

"I'm on the Falkland Islands!"

"Oh," she said, her face dropping as if he had uttered an inappropriate word. "What are you doing there?"

"Searching for my dad."

"Okay, right. Yes, I remember, what a tragedy that was. Have you found anything?"

"Not really."

"By the way, how is Frank? I still think of him sometimes. Is he okay?"

"Well, he's on the islands with me right now."

"Wow, that I was not expecting." She sounded genuinely shocked.

"How's Auntie Kay?" she asked hesitantly.

"She died about ten months ago."

"Sorry to hear that, Kev," he could tell by the blank look on her face that she was puzzled by the conversation and waiting for him to reveal the real reason for getting in contact.

"Not to worry, Pat. Look, I know it's a long shot, but the reason I wanted to contact you was because I wondered if Frank ever mentioned anything about my parents, you know, after the war?"

"Wow," she mumbled, clearly shocked by the unexpected question. "It was a long time ago, Kevin, but no, sorry. I don't remember Frank ever mentioning anything much about them."

"I know it was a long time ago, but I'm desperate. Anything you can think of that might help. Maybe something Frank mentioned in passing?"

"Well, I do remember he told me once that your dad's death was bad enough, but it was your mum's death that really finished him off."

"Oh? In what way?"

"Well, yes, you know, with the suicide and everything?"

"Suicide? What suicide?"

"I mean the *suicide*, Kevin. You know...the shock of it at the time?"

Kevin felt like someone had just shoved a sock down in his throat. "What do you mean, Pat? Who committed suicide?"

"Your mum, of course! You must have known that?"

"My mum died of cancer, didn't she?"

Suddenly Pat went quiet. Her face changed to a white colour as if the life had drained from her. "Kev," she howled. "I don't understand. Did you not know?"

Anger overwhelming him, Kevin felt unable to reply. *Why hadn't anyone told me the truth?*

"I'm so sorry. I just assumed that you of all people knew."

"I've got to go," he managed to mumble. "Sorry, Pat. I'll call you back."

He couldn't talk anymore. Trying to assemble his thoughts, he turned off his laptop and closed it shut.

Lies and more lies.

Frank Drysdale—the man who had lied to him for years, who had hidden his shot wounds from him. The man whose version of events could never be trusted.

The more he thought about it, the more sinister his thoughts became. He realised that Frank had not been telling the truth the whole time. Worse still, he had made it more difficult for Kevin to find out the truth about his parents. Not only had he hidden the truth about his mother's death from him, but worse still, he had misled him about his father. He had left out all the clues that might have helped him find things that really mattered, like that 2 PARA had witnessed the tragedy at Fitzroy, an omission obviously relevant to his father's disappearance. He had concocted some ridiculous theory about his father being in the SAS. All the little details that might have helped Kevin with his search for clues, Frank seemed to have carelessly omitted or changed.

This was the man who had admitted killing Auntie Kay. Suddenly, he felt there was something very sinister going on. Yes, Frank Drysdale was not who he claimed to be. It was now not too improbable to think that this man also had something to do with his father's death.

Had Frank killed his father and spent the rest of his life since, feigning mental illness, loss of memory, in order to get away with it?

Kevin froze. He was so angry. He felt duped and conned. No wonder the bastard had turned off his phone, because he knew his adopted son was getting closer to the truth.

But not answering the phone was not going to stop him. He was going to find Frank. It was time to find out the truth before it was too late.

Yes, it was time for the truth. Time for confrontation.

He got up and walked out of his hotel room.

Chapter 29

"What are you thinking about, Frank?" asked Fiona softly, seated next to him on a bar sofa. She was huddled up as close as possible, holding his hand and staring at him affectionately with her concerned blue eyes as they sat in the corner of the bar.

"Not much. Just enjoying the moment!" Frank replied.

It was true, the interior of The Stanley Arms, the old-fashioned bar made of oak wooden panels, reminded him of the old days when bars were about atmosphere and tradition rather than prices and trends. Being in this special bar with his new girlfriend, he felt so content, a feeling he had forgotten, that feeling of living with a purpose.

As Fiona continued to smile at him proudly, he recollected on the day so far. It had been an emotional journey back to Port Stanley. As he and Jack sat together on the flight back, Jack had opened up about his own experiences from the war, about his experiences in Stanley when the islands were invaded, how his life had been irrevocably turned upside down by the unwelcome Argentinean invaders. How, thanks to his own experiences back in 1982, he too also suffered with nightmares and panic attacks.

Frank felt embarrassed as he listened. He had been so absorbed in his own problems that he had blanked out all the others who had suffered. It made him determined to cut the self-pity and try to think of others.

Once they made it back, they had met Fiona at the Victory Bar. After the emotional day, he had been overjoyed to see her again, reminded of how much he needed her presence and smile. Her appearance was a sight for his sore and weary eyes. She was all dressed up in vibrant colours— lovely bright red, tight trousers and a white shirt covered with a bright blue sweater. She lit up his mood like a rainbow, and it only made the day so far even more surreal. That's why he was feeling so sentimental, unable to get the emotions of the day away but also proud of his progress.

Earlier, Jack had left them, promising to meet up later and, as they sat in the quiet Victory Bar, Frank had expressed his desire to Fiona to visit more of the bars in Port Stanley and do what he called a "pub crawl," drinking a beer in each of the bars in town. That was when he found out from the locals that there were actually more bars in this tiny plot of land than back home in the much larger village of Tayport.

The Stanley Arms was the fourth bar they had visited so far, and the one Frank liked most. It looked more like an old-fashioned town hall than any drinking establishment. It was also a long way out of the centre, west, past the government house. Inside, perhaps because there were fewer tourists, the atmosphere was more serene. Whatever the reason, the smiling faces and calm chatter helped erase the earlier dramas of the day.

"Fiona, are you like this with all veterans?" he asked her with a glint in his eye. He knew it wasn't true, that he was just teasing her, but perhaps part of him also wanted to know what was causing her to behave in this loving way.

Why him? It was a need for confirmation—his insecurity made him need to know that these feelings she had were real. Perhaps he sensed a bit of trepidation that he was heading home in a few days and this was a last attempt at clarity, however painful.

As expected, Fiona had no difficulty understanding the double meaning of his question. "Woah. Insecure, aren't you?" She smiled. "Er no, Frank. I don't usually throw myself over people. I'm actually quite reserved and shy!"

"Really?"

"I know, it confuses a lot of people, but yeah, some people just bring out the best in me. In fact, I haven't had a boyfriend for years."

"You haven't?"

"If you want me to be honest, there's something I like about you. You're like a lost soul."

"A lost soul?" he asked, unsure what she meant.

"Yeah, it's like looking in a mirror sometimes. I see a reflection of me. Like meeting myself, a lost soul like me."

"I never thought of you as a lost soul, Fiona," Frank said softly.

"This bravado is just a mask, Frank, an act," she said, moving closer as if to hide her face.

Frank put his hands under her chin and lifted her face up gently. He saw tears streaming down her face.

"Frank, I never told anyone this before, but I have post-traumatic stress too."

"You do?"

"Can I tell you? Would you listen?"

"Of course, Fi," Frank said quietly, squeezing her hands for comfort.

"I was only eight when war broke out, but I remember it all like it was yesterday. My father was a doctor, so we had to stay on the islands. A lot of other people got offers and were flown to the UK, but a few of us stayed. My parents refused to leave, actually." Fiona stopped, the memory causing her to grimace. For a moment, she was no longer able to look at him. Instead, she stared blankly past him.

Frank recognised that lost look in himself.

"Frank, have you seen that film *The Sound of Music*?"

"You mean the kids movie with Julie Andrews?"

"Yes."

"Well, I used to watch it in the late sixties when I was a little kid."

"Well, don't laugh, but I've always felt a strong connection with that film."

"Why?"

"Well, I was going through the same thing as the kids in the film. You know, in the film, the Germans invaded Austria. It made me understand that I wasn't alone, my home had been invaded and all that. Also in the film, they managed to run away and escape, running away to Switzerland."

"Did you run away too?"

"Eventually, when I was nineteen, I ran away to Chile. I got an English teaching job there and then after a while"—she let out a barely audible sigh—"I got stuck in a bad marriage."

"Oh."

"Yeah." She grimaced at the memory. "Not ready to go there yet, Frank."

"I'm sorry, Fiona."

"Let's talk about something else."

"Okay," Frank said softly. He didn't want the evening to end on a sad note like this. He wanted to push away the dark feelings, not think about where this relationship might be heading, and yet he also knew it was also the right time for him to open up too. "I've got a little secret too, Fiona."

"Oh?" she cooed.

Frank loved the look of innocence on her face, like a child.

"Go on then, tell me, Mr. Drysdale. Let's have it!"

"I'm half English."

"Oh?" Her face was a mixture of relief that it wasn't something more serious. "I noticed Kevin's accent was stronger, but..."

"I'm originally from Newcastle. My dad came from there, but my mum was from Scotland. We lived in Newcastle until I was about twelve."

"What happened then?"

"My dad lost his job and so my parents decided to move up to Tayport where my mum came from. My dad eventually got a job in the shipyards in Dundee."

Suddenly, Frank stopped and composed himself. He wanted so much to tell her how he missed Newcastle, the iconic architecture and the bridges that crossed the River Tyne, but he was afraid of getting too emotional if he continued. Perhaps it was the fear of crying that, once he started, he would be unable to stop. It was a kind of defence mechanism he had always employed, but never had he felt the fear so strongly.

Newcastle.

That was the last time he had cried, leaving his beloved Newcastle as he sat in the back of the family car. He had always felt he belonged there because that's where he was happiest, where all the nice memories of holidays on Whitley Bay's golden sandy beaches had occurred. Even after all these years, just thinking about those early years made him emotional. As if wanting to divert his emotions, he leaned over and kissed Fiona on the cheek.

"Fiona, I want to tell you thank you."

"Thank you? For what?" Fiona smiled innocently.

"For making me happy."

"You make me happy too, Frank."

Though it pleased him to hear that, Frank wasn't sure how to proceed. Explaining his feelings had never been his strong point. "It's just, everyone goes out of their way to make me feel welcome," he continued awkwardly. "I know people mean well, but it's very strange to be on the receiving end...you know. Back home, it feels like nobody gives a fuck. A lot of people say we asked for it, that it was our job, that we signed up for it. Maybe it was like that for some of them, but it wasn't like that for me. I only joined the army because it was an opportunity. An escape. From my family. I never wanted to go to war, but anyway, what I meant to say was thanks."

"We are grateful, Frank, that's all. None of us here have ever forgotten the British sacrifice made to free us. And we never will."

"You know," Frank said, unable to stop now, as if Fiona had given him permission to keep pouring his heart out. "Someone once told me that more Falklands veterans have been lost to suicide than the casualties during the war. When we went home, nobody took care of us or stopped to thank us." He suddenly went quiet, shocked by the emotion pouring out of him.

"It's okay to be bitter, Frank," said Fiona encouragingly, now clearly trying to sober up. "But you can't blame people for not understanding what it was like."

"It's just that until my trip here, I always felt nobody cared. Back home, I'm just a statistic, some loner who spends most of his day in a pub, drinking beer."

"What about when you got home? Weren't there people waiting to greet you?"

"Not for me personally. For others maybe, but it didn't mean anything. None of them had experienced real war. They had just watched it unfolding on the TV. The public couldn't understand that the media was controlled and all that. They never really knew what was really going on."

"Frank, like I said, you just can't expect people to under-stand war. Not even those who have been to war under-stand it, so what chance have the public got?"

Frank stooped. The truth of that hit him. Shut him up. *Yeah, that is true*, he thought. *Decades later and I still don't get what war is about.*

"Frank, I was wondering. I have a question, but you don't have to answer if you don't want to."

"No, ask me. I don't mind."

"Were you in the battle of Wireless Ridge?"

Frank froze, but though the timing of the question shocked him, he knew she was the only person in the world who could ask such a question and it seemed selfish not to respond when she had already told him so much of her own personal stuff.

"It's just that Jack said you were helping 2 PARA, so I figured..."

"Yes, I was there." Frank took a deep breath. "Apparently, anyway." He smiled, knowing how strange his answer sounded.

"Apparently?"

"Well, it's just that I don't remember it, any of it. Why did you want to know?"

"Because I remember watching some of the battle from my bedroom window."

"Oh?" was all Frank could say. He wondered how much she had seen so many miles away. "You can't see Wireless Ridge from the town, can you?"

"Yeah, it's not as far as you think. I'll show you when we walk back."

"But what do you remember?"

"Funny, but even though I was so young, I remember thinking it was just another horrible, frightening, tough, noisy day after many other horrible and frightening, tough, noisy days. But that day, I felt the war was getting very close. That evening, while putting up the blackouts, we stood at that window for a very long time and returned to it several more times that sleepless night. Watching the colours and lights of the battle. Some eerie bright bursts lit up the sky and ground, casting shadows amongst the rocks. Others traced angry colourful arcs across the sky. We'd watched the battles in the slightly more distant mountains, but I'd never noticed the colours of the tracers before. Perhaps the larger distance hid them from sight. This time they were close and bright."

"My God," Frank gasped, amazed at the power of her memory. The memory of an eight-year-old. She had been so young, it seemed so unfair that she had to experience war.

"We knew the boggy, rocky layout well," she continued, oblivious to his thoughts. "Tried to think about the men up there in the dark, fighting for our freedom. They had mums and homes and families too. Between the noise of the large enemy guns, we could hear the sounds of the British weapons. Short bursts of fire. Longer, heavier bursts. Huge bangs. At one point, Dad identified tanks as being there too."

"There were tanks?" Frank said. "I had no idea."

"Really? You don't remember anything at all?"

"People never believe me, but it's true. I remember absolutely nothing. Actually, there is something I remembered recently, vaguely. A feeling of déjà vu."

"What do you mean?"

"It's just that, since I came back here to Stanley, I get this feeling when I look out of the hotel window...I just get the sense that I've been here before."

"Well, maybe you have."

"No, not possible!"

"Why not?"

"Because I was shot on Wireless and then taken to the SS *Uganda.* I'm sure of it now. I was never in Port Stanley." Frank could hear his voice getting louder and immediately regretted it.

Fiona was about to say something, but then she hesitated and stayed silent. As if by strength, she dried her eyes, sat up and gave Frank the broadest smile somebody had ever given him.

That was the moment he felt brave. He pulled her towards him and gave her a long kiss. Closing his eyes, he put his arms around her and squeezed her as tightly as he could, not wanting to ever let her go. As she kissed him back, he opened his eyes and looked around him to savour the moment.

That was the moment he spotted someone standing by the front door of the bar. There was something familiar about him. A man he had seen before, wearing normal casual clothes. He gasped as he tried to process what he was looking at.

It was his old friend, Baz Turner.

Too shocked to move, he struggled to process how Baz might still be alive or how he might have found his way here, to this particular bar. How could he be alive? How would he still be on the islands after all this time? How was that possible? He saw that Baz was staring straight at him, his gaze a disapproving glare of disgust and anger. He wondered if he was in some kind of nightmare and now seeing the ghost of Baz. Sometimes, when he was tired, he would see things that weren't there, but this time was different. This was really happening. This was no ghost. This couldn't be another flashback. It was too real.

Baz continued to stare angrily at him as if to say, "You think it's enough to go to a cemetery? And now you're pissing about with the local women? How dare you enjoy yourself? How dare you sit there without a care in the world, getting drunk. You tell the world how much you miss me and yet look at you, sitting there drinking. Is this how you choose to remember me?"

As Frank stared back at him, he felt so betrayed. All these years, Baz had been alive, living on the islands. Why hadn't he said anything? Why had he put his wife, Angie, through the torment of believing he was dead? What hurt most was that there was no smile after thirty-nine years, only contempt. The injustice tore at him and made it impossible for him to breathe.

"What is it, Frank? Are you okay?" Frank could hear Fiona's voice to his right. "Frank, are you okay?"

But he could not reply. Instead, Frank began to panic, suddenly feeling claustrophobic and dizzy.

"What is it, Frank. Talk to me." Fiona was now talking a bit louder, pleading.

The bar had turned silent, the landlord looking very concerned.

Not knowing where to look, Frank turned his head away from the door in shame. "I need to go outside," he managed to whisper, now looking firmly at the floor. He could feel himself being supported, arms holding him up as his legs gave way. He could hear a scuffle as people moved out of the way or rushed to help. Only the music in the background and the scraping sound of his boots on the floor as they dragged him off could be heard now.

He reached out his arms as if to ask Baz for forgiveness, but as he got nearer the door, he looked up and realised it was too late.

Baz had disappeared.

That was the moment he passed out.

ACCEPTANCE

Chapter 30

As soon as Frank's senses slowly began to return, he knew was no longer in the pub. He was lying down on his back, looking up at the clear black sky, marvelling at the stars and how they seemed to partly hide behind the orange stripes of the evening sunset.

As the cold night air blew on his face, he heard Fiona talking to him and tilted his head sideways to see her crying, her eyes scared and concerned.

"Honey, you okay?"

"I saw him," he muttered, sure that this time he had not had a flashback or imagined it, that he had really seen his friend.

"You saw who?" Fiona said, frustrated that she was unable to understand.

Embarrassed, he willed himself to get back on his feet. Luckily, he was not in physical pain, but he noticed a small crowd of people standing near the open door, giving him funny looks. He wondered if these islanders had become used to overemotional veterans visiting the islands, reliving their traumas, prone to emotional wobbles.

"What happened, Frank?" Fiona said as he sat down on the nearest bench.

"I'm sure I saw my mate."

"What mate? Where?"

"My mate, Baz. By the door."

"By the door? Is this the friend you had from the war?"

"Yes, how did you know?" He had told her so many things about his past, but he was certain he had never mentioned Baz.

"Jack mentioned him briefly, said he was Kevin's father, right?"

"Yeah, look, it was nothing. I'm sorry."

"I'm sorry too, Frank. I had too many beers, so I was a bit slow to react."

"It wasn't your fault, Fiona."

"Tell me about him, Frank."

He looked her in the eyes, ready to tell her, ignoring the lump in his throat. "He was my mate. He was in 2 PARA. I followed him into the army...you know...but he never came home."

"What happened?"

"Nobody knows, but I still think about him all the time. Fiona, I know it sounds really silly, but it's not possible he was here, is it?"

"What was his last name?"

"Turner."

"Well, I've been living here all my life and I'm pretty sure there is no Baz Turner on these islands."

"What if he changed his name?" Frank said, desperate for something to make sense. The person who resembled Baz had looked so real.

"Why would he do that?"

Frank knew she was making sense. He knew he had been prone to flashbacks and nightmares over the last few months—it never seemed to stop. He had made so much progress in the last few months, trying to address all his problems and attempting to fix them by travelling thousands of miles. What was the point? What had he achieved? Any progress he had made seemed so futile because Baz was still tormenting him. Would he ever be free from the guilt, the black cloud that followed him around? How much longer could he take the constant reminders, the unforgiving whine of his friend's ghost?

"Yeah, you're right, sorry. It's just that he never goes away. I kind of hoped that after today, you know, going to all those graves and paying my respects, he would finally leave me alone."

"Come on, Frank, let's take a walk."

It seemed like a good idea, and Frank nodded his head. He hoped the fresh air might help him get his bearings back. Someone had already been back inside the pub to fetch their coats, and as he put his thick coat on, he felt properly protected against the now cold, biting wind.

They walked westwards down the main street, holding hands, past the racecourse. Neither said a word for a few minutes.

"Frank, you know I have survivor's guilt too?"

"You? Why would you have survivor's guilt, Fiona?"

"It's hard to explain, but I've always felt unworthy because of the war."

"How do you mean?"

"So many people died because of us...us little people living on an unknown faraway island. I mean, I was only eight years old, but every day I think to myself, was I worth it? Did I really deserve to be freed? Was there something I could have done to stop all the deaths?"

"I hadn't thought of that, Fiona."

"Anyway, Frank," she said in a solemn and sympathetic tone. She stopped walking and touched him on his shoulder.

Frank stopped too.

"This guy Baz was your mate, right? So, he would want the best for you, just like I want the best for you, right? Baz would not want you to spend your life feeling guilty, would he? He would be happy that you survived, that you took care of his son. Right?"

"Guess so." As Frank spoke, he felt so grateful that Fiona was here listening and understanding.

In the past, there had always been a feeling of insecurity in finding a friend. Finding love or friendship almost inevitably meant loss at some point. Good things never lasted, and people died, so he had always shied away from getting too close to anyone. For years, he had been cold and bad tempered, keeping things close to himself. That was how he had always lived before, running away from the truth, keeping it in and praying that somehow everything would just go away. But right now, he felt different. Today had taught him that time was precious. In a few days, he would be leaving Fiona and Jack and going back home. Peace may have returned to these islands, but the war inside himself would continue. He had to use his remaining time to try and make peace with himself too, and part of that was admitting his mistakes.

"I should have done what we did today years ago, Fiona," Frank continued. "I sort of realised this today, being in that cemetery at San Carlos. It's like all these years, I've been hiding, living in a shell."

"Of course, Frank. Everyone does that."

"But shit, I was so young." Frank sighed heavily. "I was only seventeen." He began to shiver slightly, and his chest heaved. "I just wanted to see the world. I was just a kid."

"Isn't that part of why you came back, right? To offload your past, come face to face with it?"

"Yeah?"

"So, let's do that together! Let's finish what you came here to do, hold your head up high and be proud."

There was a moment of silence. Frank wanted to walk again, thinking it was too cold to stand still. In the background, he could hear logger ducks, their unique sounds exclusive to this part of the world, and the sounds of oyster catchers in their boats drifting over towards him from the harbour, and the faint sounds of cars. Maybe he felt desperate because he knew their relationship was doomed. Eight thousand miles wasn't just a long way to go to war. It was also a long distance to be in love. How could their relationship possibly survive when they lived so far apart?

Doomed or not, he felt like a teenager again and he grabbed her, pulling her towards him, and kissed her. Unable to breathe, he closed his eyes. "Fiona," he whispered, "I love you."

"I love you too, Frank," she whispered back urgently, unwilling to let go of him.

Frank knew that to finish their kiss would be like returning to reality, back to the mundane world where all their troubles lay, where all their problems were patiently waiting for them.

Eventually he managed to let go and open his eyes, expecting to see Baz nearby, disapproving, but instead, as he looked past Fiona, the remains of the orange sunset still scarred the evening air and thousands of stars punctured the cloudless sky, lighting the landscape up in the distance. But it was the red lights that blinked in the far distance that grabbed his attention. The same feeling of déjà vu he'd had the first night he had looked out of his hotel window and the night he looked out of the hospital window. The feeling that he had been to Port Stanley before. Except this time, he understood what it was.

The lights of Port Stanley.

He had seen these lights before, flickering in the distance. It was still a few miles away in the darkness, but he remembered the last time he had been there, sitting on the ridge in the distance and watching in awe at the view of Stanley. He remembered the endless blue of the sea and the clearness of the dark sky filled with thousands of stars. But most of all, he remembered the lights of Stanley illuminating the town of red and green roofed houses.

From Wireless Ridge.

"What is it, Frank?" Fiona asked.

Frank turned to look at her. "Fiona, please. I need you to do me a favour," he said quietly, pointing his finger westwards. "Is that Wireless Ridge over there?"

"Yes, Frank. I was going to show you, remember? We talked about it in the pub. Why?"

Frank froze. Up there on Wireless Ridge somewhere was where his lost memory lay. Up there was where all the answers lay, the final frontier, the final puzzle pieces. It was a long walk away, but it was a walk he had to do. He had to know the truth. Only up there would he find the answers that would help him find peace.

"Fiona, I want you to do something for me. It's my last wish before I leave."

Fiona listened, nodded her head, then got her mobile from her jacket and made a call.

Chapter 31

Finding Frank turned out to be a far harder job than Kevin had anticipated. Determined to confront him with questions about his parents and his lies, he had left the hotel an hour ago and headed for the Victory Bar only to find that Frank was not there but on a pub crawl around Port Stanley with Fiona.

Eventually, after a long trail, Kevin ended up on the west side of town, outside a bar called The Stanley Arms. Even after the long and unexpected walk across town, he still seethed with anger. For years, Frank had hidden from him that his mother killed herself. All the other lies over the years about the shot wound, the dodgy memory, the drunk behaviour that had caused Auntie Kay to have died.

But his anger quickly dissipated as he opened the door and walked in. The place was full, but he spotted Frank immediately on a sofa near the bar, sitting with Fiona. She was laughing with him, kissing and cuddling him. Having spent the last hour wanting to kill the guy, Kevin was suddenly disarmed by his happiness. It seemed the wrong place and time to confront him with these serious allegations. He was about to turn around and leave when Frank looked up and their eyes met. In that moment, time seemed to freeze. A look of a thousand emotions reflected in Frank's face. As he blinked, his eyes seemed to cloud over with a mixture of shock and surprise as though he was unable to process what he was seeing. It was the "lost in the woods" look Kevin had seen so many times before, except today it was more intense than it had ever been. It was a look that was specially reserved for Kevin. In that split second, all its associations of abandonment, jealousy and resentment came back from Kevin's past.

It was like someone had pushed pause and time was standing still. Bad memories of his upbringing came rushing back. Frank's drunken aggression towards Auntie Kay, the tension that filled the house for days after violent incidents, the arguing. Most of all, that haunted look he had just witnessed, like Frank's spirit had left the room and you were left looking at an empty human vessel. Suddenly, confronting Frank with the issues of his father's whereabouts no longer mattered. He turned around and ran back to the hotel.

Even after a ten-minute sprint back to the hotel, Kevin's confusion continued. His head pinged with endless questions. He lay down on the bed and tried to recompose himself. He was so angry that his hands were still shaking as he grabbed his laptop and opened Facebook messenger.

He noticed an unread message from Dave Townsend.

"Hi, Kev. I've found out a bit more about your dad when you are ready."

"Hi, Dave, I'm here!"

"Unfortunately, most of it is rumour and hearsay."

"I understand that."

The veteran wrote about how everyone loved his dad, respected him. How, when he got injured, he was sent to Ajax Bay, but after that, the trail went cold. Nobody Dave spoke to had seen him at Fitzroy. "I'm pretty sure someone would have mentioned it if they had," Dave wrote. "But, as I told you before, there was a lot of shit going on at the time with *Galahad* and all that. There were so many rumours, like that he fled to Chile or Argentina. Most of them assumed he'd died as he made his way to Fitzroy."

"Thanks, Dave. There's one thing I don't get, though. Why cover it up, why did the government refuse to say anymore?"

"I can only say that everyone was really upset about the silence. I think some guys took it to court, but it didn't get far. I can only say that a lot of stuff about what was going on in the war was covered up quietly."

"Oh? What sort of things?"

"Things like the fact that the British used phosphorous grenades despite them being banned by the Geneva convention. But also, other stuff like people losing it with prisoners, people quietly demoted because of their behaviour. Stuff like 'blue on blue' incidents, secret missions...it's a long list. However, most of us agree that covering up whatever happened to your dad was unnecessary. It certainly hasn't made the issue go away. It's more that we are powerless to do anything."

"Well, I've got a lawyer on it."

"Good luck with that, Kevin. Maybe with the fortieth anniversary coming up, you never know, maybe it is time. By the way, I've also got some info on Frank Drysdale, if you want it."

Kevin sighed. What had happened to Frank seemed so unimportant right now. Once again, the trail to his father's last known whereabouts had gone cold, the answers as far away as they always had been. The only person who might know anything, Frank, was clearly too traumatised to ever be in a position to remember anything. Maybe it was time to give up. Maybe it was better this way. At least he had tried. Perhaps he had been too ambitious to see the impossible task he faced. But at the very least, he had come back here and walked in his father's last footsteps. He had to try and take some comfort from that.

"Nah, not now. I'm feeling numb right now, but thank you so much, Dave."

"Are you sure? I've been talking to a few guys who served with him. They heard rumours about how he was shot."

"Oh?" Suddenly Kevin perked up. After all the lies, maybe knowing some of the truth about Frank might cheer him up. "Okay!" he typed.

"Rumour has it, he was shot by a prisoner with a pistol on Wireless Ridge."

It took a few seconds for him to digest the answer. He remembered the doctor at the hospital telling him Frank was shot with a pistol, but having it finally confirmed still confused him. If he had been shot by a prisoner, then why the secrecy? Was it really so shameful to be shot by a prisoner? Most of all, he struggled to understand how Frank could have possibly forgotten such an incident. Or had he not forgotten but was too ashamed to admit it?

After a minute, Dave typed, "You still there, Kev?"

"Yeah. Why a pistol?"

"Well, most of the enemy officers had pistols. Apparently, it was how they controlled the conscripts. They weren't really any use in combat situations."

"Dave, I really appreciate all your help," he typed.

It was at this moment that Kevin's mobile rang, startling him. It was his lawyer calling. He answered, "Hi—"

"Okay, look. About the Ministry of Defence, we are not making progress with your dad, I'm afraid." The lawyer was not in the mood for small talk. He sounded worried and concerned.

It didn't surprise Kevin to hear that.

"Their stance is that to reveal what they knew about your dad would endanger other activities going on at the time. It's too sensitive, they said, best left alone. They added that as his body was never found or identified, the main issue would remain unresolved."

"Unresolved?"

"Yeah, nobody knows where he is. That's what they claim."

"Okay."

"However, we did make other progress."

"Oh?" Suddenly Kevin felt hope again.

"I applied to the Ministry of Defence for military records about Frank, but they said that as long as Frank is alive, any details would remain protected. However, I was able to get in touch with a veteran who was privy to the information, off the record, of course."

"What did you find out then?"

"We know why he never made it to Port Stanley."

"Well, I know that too. He was shot!"

"Yes, at Wireless Ridge, that's right, but do you know how he was shot, Kevin?"

"Yes, I was just talking to a veteran from 2 PARA. He said the rumours were that he was shot by a prisoner with a pistol?"

"Well, that's not the whole story, Kevin, I'm afraid."

"What do you mean? What is this?"

"I don't know how to explain this, but…"

"For God's sake, tell me!"

"Frank wasn't shot by a prisoner after all."

As the lawyer finally blurted out the truth, Kevin went white and screamed.

Chapter 32

As Jack drove Frank and Fiona up the dirt tracks, towards the top of Wireless Ridge, Frank knew there was no turning back. Whatever was up on that ridge, he had to face it. Tomorrow would be too late, for then his bottle would be gone. The thought of returning to Scotland not knowing what happened to him on Wireless Ridge was not an option.

Twenty minutes earlier, realising the significance of seeing the lights of Stanley, he had pleaded with Fiona to help him get up to the ridge. Thankfully, instead of dismissing Frank's suggestion with excuses that it was too dark or cold, Fiona had rung Jack. Eventually, Jack had arrived in a 4 X 4 with some extra clothes and beers and was now ferrying them up towards Wireless Ridge.

As they ascended the dirt tracks, the shadow of a large metal cross, a brass plaque recording the names of those killed in the battle, loomed over them. Finally, as they reached the top, the car stopped.

"So, you remember seeing the lights of Stanley from the ridge?" Jack said, turning around.

"Yeah."

"Just that I thought there wouldn't be any lights on back then. Thought they would have been turned off or the windows would have been boarded up."

"No, they were definitely on. I clearly remember looking down from the ridge and seeing them. Maybe I remember it because there was something surreal about them."

"How do you mean?"

"Well, finally seeing Port Stanley was like the end of a long journey. The last destination of the war was finally within view."

"Kind of like seeing the top of Mount Everest, you mean?"

"Sort of."

"Anyway, Frank, you sure you want to do this? It's not too late to turn back," Jack said.

"I have to do this, Jack. I must," replied Frank in a whisper, squeezing Fiona's hand.

"Okay. I will sit and wait in the car for you both, alright?" said Jack. "Remember, it's really cold out there, so we can't stay too long or you will freeze."

Frank nodded, and he and Fiona got out. As they walked off, Frank deliberately walked past the cross, ignoring it. Time was in short supply and, after the visit to San Carlos earlier in the day, he wasn't ready for more remembrance.

After a minute of walking, they paused for breath. He could no longer hear the engine of the car running in the background. They were completely alone on the ridge.

Holding Fiona's hand tightly, he turned around to see the unspoiled views of the mountains in the distance. Once they had been battlefields—Two Sisters, Mount Longdon, Mount Kent and Mount Tumbledown—buzzing with activity back then, but now they looked as if they had been handed back to nature. The stars lit up the outline of the mountain silhouettes.

But it was the lights of Stanley that held his attention most. Last time, it had been winter, darker and colder, but it was still the same view. The red lights of Stanley twinkled and sparkled in the distance, just as they had thirty-nine years earlier.

He looked down to his left and remembered that hidden in the darkness a long way down the ridge was the place where the battle had started. He remembered the flashback he had had at Darwin where, as the order was given to fix bayonets, he had looked up and seen the ridge where he was now standing, a saddled ridge with sides plastered with exposed rock and boulders. It had been a terrifying sight because it seemed like the perfect defensive position, with hundreds of massive granite shards littered around that looked like axe heads, perfect places for the enemy to hide behind.

As he stared into the abyss of darkness, he heard a whisper in his ear. At first, he thought it had been the wind or Fiona, but then the second time he heard it, he knew exactly what it was.

"Find the rock," the whisper said.

He froze, closing his eyes in fear of the voice from his last nightmare, on the hospital ship, SS *Uganda*.

"Frank, are you okay?" he heard Fiona ask, but the voice had taken over now.

"Find the rock, find the rock," the bandaged man from the hospital ship whispered in his ear again.

Opening his eyes, his could feel his stomach tighten and his heart thump with sheer fear.

Of course, he had to find the rock. It all made sense to him now. The rock had always been the big clue, the key to everything. The rock had all the answers to unclogging his memories. He had not found it at Darwin because it was here, somewhere down the other side of the ridge, and now, he had one last opportunity to find it.

He immediately let go of Fiona's hand and began running down the north side of the ridge. "Down there," he shouted to himself, running past the large rocks deftly.

Almost as soon as he reached the edge of the ridge, the moonlight was cut off by the sharp rocks and everything went dark. The further down he went, the more he struggled to navigate the rocky ledges and slippery surfaces. Last time he had been here, he had been a young, fit soldier, still a teenager, prepared for every obstacle that stood before him, trained and in peak fitness. Back then, he had managed to walk vast distances without sleep, without stopping, carrying unheard of weights on his back as he stomped across these islands under brutal and demanding weather conditions. But tonight, after only five minutes' descent, his body ached with exhaustion. He had to constantly stop to catch his breath as he slowly made his way down the rocky terrain. Even the weather had changed now, and the biting wind battled against his thick winter wear.

"Find the rock," he shouted to himself.

Somewhere above and behind him, he could hear Fiona's cries of panic, screaming that she couldn't see him, pleading with him to come back. But the further down he went, the more her cries seemed to fade in the wind.

And then, as he rested on a rock to catch his breath, something caught his eye to the left. An outline, a shape he had seen thousands of times in his nightmares. He squinted just to make sure his mind was not tricking him. Then he walked towards it, wanting to get nearer so he could see it closer, touch it and feel it. He rubbed his eyes and tried to focus, unable to believe what he was seeing.

It was the rock from his nightmares, the same rock he had hidden behind when he was being ambushed. He ran closer to confirm, but there was no doubt. It looked exactly how he remembered it. Two white rocks fused together halfway, the overall shape a deformed rectangle about two feet high. He noted the uneven steeply inclined formation, the sharp jagged edges and the little areas of different-coloured moss growing around it. It was no longer bright green moss, but light grey, decayed, exposed to decades of wind.

He grazed his fingers over the sharp edges. It had only been an hour since he thought he saw Baz in the pub. Was this the same kind of deception? Was he dreaming again? Was this a flashback?

Needing further affirmation, he lay down behind the wet cold rock as he had done so many times before in his dreams, poked his head around and looked up.

Yes, this was the rock. This was the exact view from the nightmares that had tormented him for decades. The same rock that he had hidden behind for cover, out of ammo, ready to die.

Ker chunk, ker chunk.

Without warning, he was lost in a flashback. The same one he'd had at Darwin, but a few minutes after he had killed the enemy soldier. He was hiding behind his rock, caught in an ambush and being pounded by artillery and mortars. The sky was lit up with explosions. The sounds were deafening, the ground shaking under the huge artillery bombardment.

Despite the noise, he could hear voices further up from where he was and made out some words of Spanish, realising it was the enemy.

Were they looking for him? Had they seen him bayonetting the enemy?

Panicking, he remembered he had no ammo, that his sub machine gun had jammed in the enemy bunker. All he had now to defend himself was the pistol he had stolen from the bayonetted soldier.

That was the moment he remembered having a phosphorus grenade in his webbing too. Without hesitating, he stood up, unpinned it and then threw it into the darkness towards the enemy voices above.

BOOM.

He had thrown the grenade. Not the enemy.

There was a huge explosion followed by an enormous flash of white light that briefly lit up the area. He knew it had hit his target because an enemy soldier was now engulfed with fire, screaming in pain and thrashing about wildly in desperation, in the hope that it would put out the fire.

Then, as Frank watched on, the enemy stopped screaming and fell down in a ball of fire, rolling down towards him before stopping a metre away from his rock. As he stared at the body, it was no longer on fire but just smouldering with a thin line of black smoke. It was blackened, beyond recognition.

Cowering in fear of what would happen next, he hid again behind the rock. That was when he saw something near the charred body. He only noticed it because it flickered in the faint moonlight with a glint. He reached out his hand, squinted his eyes and took a closer look.

It was two dog tags stuck together. The nylon string was no longer attached to it. Just a small coin size circle of aluminium. He picked it up, wiped off the dirt and read it.

OPOS
24445513
TURNER
BR
CE

He reeled with incomprehension. How was this possible? Baz was never at Wireless Ridge. He had gone to Ajax Bay, so how had he ended up here? It made no sense.

Needing time to think, he kept holding the dog tags in his hand, still staring at the engraved letters and numbers, praying it had all been a mistake.

Then the truth started to sink in. He had thrown a phosphorous grenade and it had hit not the enemy but his friend, Baz Turner. It was Baz's body that had rolled down. The leather strip that kept the dog tags attached to him must have burnt along with everything else. How else could he explain what he had seen?

Not sure what to do, he pushed the tags into some mud in a hole in the rock until it was hidden from sight, then took off his cap and ripped off his own morphine syrette and stuck it in his arm.

Yes, he would die a coward—die painlessly, quickly. Out of sight. Nobody needed to know the truth.

Feeling numb from the morphine now rushing through his bloodstream, he picked up the nearby pistol and aimed it at his temple. He had to kill himself now. He didn't want to live anymore. He had seen too much, done too many horrific things. He knew he would never be able to forever carry the guilt of accidentally killing his best friend. Once a coward, always a coward. Even in victory, he was a coward.

But he wasn't able to pull the trigger. He couldn't stop thinking of what would happen if he killed himself.

Kevin? He had promised Baz he would take care of them. *Baz's wife, Angie?* What would happen to her?

Above all, he thought of his mother. How would she survive without him? He thought of her watching the television, desperate for news of her only son. How would she suffer to know that her son had killed himself, and why? Because he was a coward?

He pulled the gun down from his head and aimed up at his stomach instead, pulling the trigger. He felt a sense of relief as the bullet entered his body, then heard a crunch as the bullet smashed his shoulder bone.

Frank woke up from his flashback screaming. As some people tried to drag him away from the rock, he tried to hold on to it, not willing to return to the real world. He remembered being placed in some kind of car and the sounds of a police siren before he passed out.

Chapter 33

"Déjà vu," Kevin muttered to himself as he sat in the waiting room.

Once more, he was in a hospital listening to a doctor lecture him on the prognosis of his adoptive father, telling him that Frank was going to be okay, that Frank had this and that, how Frank needed to rest.

Trying to take in everything the doctor was saying was made more difficult by the phone call from the lawyer earlier still playing on repeat in his head.

Some veteran had claimed off the record that Frank had not been shot by a prisoner but had shot himself. As the battle was over at this point, there had been no witnesses, but the evidence had been indicative of self-harm because not only was Frank still holding the fired pistol in his hand when he was discovered but no dead enemy was found nearby. Apparently, the timing of the incident had played a big part in the reason for covering the incident up. The war was finally over, and victorious soldiers were rushing into Stanley. There had been a lot of concern about the effect of public support should the press have been told that one of the soldiers had gone berserk and shot himself. A prompt decision had been made that to reveal the incident was not in the public interest and was unnecessary.

Luckily, after the phone call ended, Kevin was able to chat to a veteran friend of Dave Townsend's, who was able to explain the confusion in a bit more detail.

"Frank should never have been sent to the Falklands in the first place."

"What do you mean?"

"Frank was never soldier material to start with. He hadn't done P Company or anything, but on the other hand, he was young, fit and strong, and had brief medical knowledge. That's why he was picked to go to war. With hindsight, they underestimated the enemy's resolve."

"What do you mean?"

"Well, for example, nobody could have foreseen what happened at Fitzroy."

"But what does what happened at Fitzroy have to do with Frank?" Kevin typed.

"I guess that witnessing the *Galahad* disaster really pushed him over the edge."

So, Frank had witnessed the Galahad *tragedy,* Kevin thought. Then he asked, "How did he end up fighting at Wireless Ridge?"

"Well, because of the troop shortage that resulted from the disaster, 2 PARA were ordered to march again. At the time, not only had we lost the killed and wounded at Goose Green, but we had also lost a lot of men from food poisoning, broken ankles, trench foot. That's why poor Frank was ordered to rejoin 2 PARA at Wireless Ridge."

There was a short silence.

"But in retrospect, they should have left him at Fitzroy."

"Why?"

"He lost it, mate."

"How do you mean?"

"He had a breakdown. He had seen so much tragedy, he just snapped. I saw many traumatised people, but Frank really lost the plot," the veteran continued.

"You need to remember that when the battle was over, the whole war ended too. Everyone was celebrating, rushing to be the first into Port Stanley, so there were many other things to think about. I think when it happened, it was still dark. I can't remember. There were other rumours that a prisoner had shot him, but everything was hearsay."

"But what about Frank? What did he say happened?" Kevin typed, not comprehending the complexity of the incident.

"He never said anything to anyone, mate. Like I said, he had a mental breakdown, not to mention being in a lot of pain from being shot. By the time the medics found him, he was spaced out, traumatised. They said some medic must have noticed him as he had been given morphine but details were vague."

"But, if Frank was in such a bad state at Fitzroy, then why put him into the battle?"

"You need to google Bluff Cove air attacks, Kevin. It wasn't just the huge losses of soldiers through death or injury, but helicopters and landing ships were also written off. This meant not only huge shortages in troop numbers but also required a massive resource reorganisation. As Donald Rumsfeld said, 'You go to war with the army you have, not the army you want.' It was a different time, and lots of difficult decisions were made in the fog of war."

"Do you know where Frank was treated?"

"Yes, that's one thing we do know. After he was shot, he was put on the hospital ship, SS *Uganda*. From there, he was sent home to some mental hospital in England. I think it was the Woolwich."

Woolwich. Kevin's head buzzed. He remembered Frank claiming in the Victory Bar that he had left the army voluntarily, getting a PVR or something. Another lie, but he no longer cared. Kevin thanked the veteran, promising to keep this to himself. The veteran replied by saying he wished he could help more.

So that was it. Tomorrow they were flying home. It was hard not to feel disappointed. What happened to his father would remain unexplained. Money was running out—already he had told his lawyer he couldn't afford to keep him on and appeal the decision of the Ministry of Defence.

He looked up and tried to listen to the doctor, who was still talking.

"Well, the damage is done. Anyway, that's it. He will stay in this hospital until tomorrow when you will fly home. Do you have any questions, Kevin?"

"Does Frank remember anything about what happened when he was at Wireless last night?"

He had already spoken to Fiona and Jack about the incident. It had been hard not to be angry with their decision to escort Frank to Wireless Ridge after all the drama at Darwin, yet he had held back from blaming them, acknowledging that they had been very good to him since they'd arrived on these islands. It wasn't hard to see that Fiona in particular had brought about a very noticeable change in Frank over the last week.

"Nothing. All we know is what Fiona witnessed—that, without warning, he ran off looking for some rock."

It was the same behaviour he had witnessed at Darwin, when Frank had run around screaming some rubbish about some rock.

"So, what happens when we get back to the UK?"

"That will be up to Frank," the doctor said. "There will be lots of therapy options, I'm sure."

Obviously, this doctor didn't know Frank very well. Kevin smirked as he thanked the doctor and left.

As he walked out of the hospital, he smiled, appreciating the irony.

Of course, the doctor didn't know Frank well. He had known the guy forty years and still didn't know him.

Chapter 34

As soon as Frank walked onto the beach, his face lit up in surprise. He wondered if this was one of the beaches he had spotted from his plane two weeks earlier. The long stretch of gorgeous white sand and the big patches of light turquoise water certainly resembled a Caribbean beach from where he was standing. There was, he noticed straight away, something unspoilt about this place—no litter, no shops or cafes, only the fresh smell of seaweed and the sights of penguins in the distance toyed with the illusion.

Despite the beauty, it was not enough to lift his mood. This beach would be the last place he would see before the long journey home. The two-week trip was finally over. From here, Jack would drive them to the local Stanley airport from where an eight-seater FIGAS plane would fly them to Mount Pleasant and from there, they'd start the long journey home via Chile.

Luckily, his second hospital stay on the islands had been short and made bearable by the constant presence of Fiona. Not only was she allowed to stay in his room all the time, but it had given them both a good opportunity to talk about what had occurred up on Wireless. Frank had already apologised many times, truthfully telling her he didn't remember much of what happened, only running down the ridge, trying to find the rock. Somehow, discussing the events with her had made him realise that the past didn't matter anymore. He had tried to address it and failed. Now it was time to put the past where it really belonged and focus on the future. As he saw it, Dr. Price had been wrong to believe that facing the past was the best way to help trauma. The truth was subjective, and it only complicated things. How could you address the truth when the mind made up so much? Memories were nothing but edited recollections.

Fiona had wanted to go somewhere special for their last moments together, so she had asked Jack to drive them down to Surf Bay, five minutes from the capital. Even after twenty minutes of walking of silence, neither of them wanted to disturb the silence, not wanting to address what was coming as the clock slowly ticked away.

Eventually, Frank managed to break the silence. "Let's hope Omicron is not bad."

"What's that?"

"Fi, don't you ever read the news?"

"No, not lately anyway."

"It's the new strain of COVID that's now going around in Europe. It came from Africa apparently."

Fiona seemed to gesture for him to stop, that she had something more important to discuss. "Frank, you know, despite everything you've told me, I haven't once seen you cry? Why not? I would not think any less of you if you did."

"I don't know. Maybe it was my upbringing, Fi. I was always taught to hold it in, that crying was for wimps, you know. Maybe I'm just too scared."

"Too scared?"

"Yeah, it's a fear I have. If I started, I would never be able to stop?"

"Well, my doctor taught me crying can be cleansing. He told me it kills bacteria, improves your moods, relieves stress. Anyway, promise me whatever happens, you'll stay in touch and look forward. The future is what matters, Frank."

Frank nodded. "Yeah, like I said yesterday, it's not always possible to make peace with my past. Whatever might have happened or didn't happen, it's just a war in my mind. There is no peace."

"Yeah, I know what you mean. Frank, listen to this. I found it on the *Guardian* website today. It´s written by Stewart Dakers. Listen. 'At other times, provoked by an old letter, a snatch of a tune, or a waft of custard or cabbage,' " Fiona read aloud from her phone. " 'I set out in hope down memory lane, where I walk my blue remembered hills, eager to find again that land of lost content, a smile on my face ready to greet a past companion, only to find there is no smile in return. Instead, I witness my younger self walking by on the other side or engaged in some act of malevolence, spite, betrayal, something that may even have changed another's life, and I want to seek pardon, but they have vanished, and I am left to wonder. But I can do more than wonder.

'For all its discomforts, the country of the past needs to be visited. I may not be able to put things right, to make amends, but I can learn from those memories. The mistakes I have made, the follies, the falsehoods, the failures, these are signposts. They show me where I must go now, what I must do. I may not have much time left, but while I may not be able to repair past damage, I can commit myself to atonement. I do not have to be condemned by the years.' "

There was a pause as Frank tried to understand what she had said.

"It's about finding peace with yourself, Frank."

"The only peace I ever found was you, Fiona," he whispered softly.

Fiona moved her hand to her mouth and started to cry. Not sure what to do, he held her close, feeling her sobs as they shook her body. He looked out to the sea, not wanting to think or feel.

As they started to walk back to Jack's car, Fiona grabbed his hand and smiled. "What music do you like, Frank?"

"Oh, I don't know. It's been years since I listened to music, really."

"Well, what used to be your favourite music, you know, when you were growing up?"

"Dire Straits."

"I know them. Which album?"

"You wouldn't know it, I don't think. It's called 'Making Movies.' "

"Why that album?"

"Because it reminds me of when I was a teenager, before I moved to Scotland, before all my troubles started. About 1980. There was this one song called 'Tunnel of Love.' Not many people know that the song is really about Newcastle in the 70s. The old Newcastle, Whitley Bay, the Spanish City. Ironically, it's all gone now, but the slow bit at the end of the song always resonated with me. When I first heard it, I had just moved up to Scotland. My dad got a new job and all that, but I was so homesick."

"I understand, Frank."

As they walked, he wanted to say more. How he still remembered the day they got in the car and left Newcastle because it was the turning point in his life. If he hadn't left Newcastle, he would never have met Baz, his dad would never have lost his job at the shipyards and turned to drink. Yet somehow, all that pain had led him down this path to Fiona.

It only took five minutes to drive to the airport from Surf Bay. He had hoped it would take a little longer and given them a few more precious moments together. Nobody spoke, but no words were necessary. It was enough that Fiona squeezed his hand tightly.

Frank cheered up briefly when he saw the airport, amused it was just a field with a small runway and a small building, but as they got out of their car and walked into the solitary building, his smile disappeared.

I'm finally going home.

He turned towards Jack. He felt so much warmth towards this man, yet he felt envious of his smile, wishing his life was as simple as it seemed to be for him.

"Goodbye, Frank," said Jack, like he had said goodbye to veterans many times before.

"Jack, thank you for all you've done for me," Frank croaked.

"No problem, Frank. Come back again when you're ready."

"I will."

"You will always be welcome here, Frank. Always," he said, then politely stepped to the side.

Frank saw a crying Fiona moving towards him and his heart sank. They had already discussed what the future held in the hospital yesterday. Fiona had talked about sending him money for another visit or her coming to visit UK, but with the world threatened by a new strain of COVID, it was going to take a while before they would meet again.

Now the moment had come, he felt he was drowning in the sea, only this time there was nobody to throw him a lifejacket.

"This is for you, Frank," she sobbed. In her hands was a wrapped up, small package.

"Fi, you shouldn't have."

"Jack helped me find this."

"What is it?" he said, opening the small box.

"It's a special necklace, two bits of a heart. It's like the one Baz had?"

Frank was unsure how to react. He expected the reminder of Baz's necklace to depress him, but instead, as he stared at the beautiful silver locket and the lovingly engraved words, "Fiona & Frank Always," he embraced it. This was the real thing, not some imaginary necklace made up by his brain. This was something he could touch anytime he wanted, his eyes could see it, and every time he did so, he would take comfort in the reminder of Fiona, a real person who loved him and wanted the best for him.

"It's beautiful, Fi," he said, as she leaned forward clumsily, nervously splitting up the heart in two and putting his part around his neck.

Feeling inadequate, he put his hand in his pocket and brought out an unwrapped ring.

"A ring with a love heart. Thank you, Frank. I will wear it and always think of you," Fiona said as she slipped it onto her finger.

"Frank, I've got you something else," she said, handing over a small, wrapped present. "Open this when you are on the plane. I wrote some instructions too. If you have any problems, then ask someone."

He looked briefly at it and put it in his pocket. Right at that moment, it could have been a million-dollar cheque or the deed to a house and he wouldn't have cared. All he knew was that his heart was about to burst as he turned back and looked into her tear-filled, kind blue eyes.

As they hugged for the last time, even Frank was surprised by his inability to cry. Perhaps it was something to do with it being too public, too open, that people were watching, yet in that moment he had never felt sadder in his whole life.

"Thank you, Fiona," he managed to murmur.

As they continued to hold each other tightly, he tried not to dwell on how his memory had failed him, that he would never know what really happened on Wireless Ridge. He was tired of the tricks his mind was playing on him, tired of trying to make sense of his shattered memories. Instead, he thought about how, in only two weeks, he had found a special love and become closer to someone than he could ever have imagined.

Despite the obvious challenges he had faced, the truth was that on these islands of hell, he had found a part of himself. He had found redemption, love, and friendship, and now he was about to lose it all. Returning to the prison where he had no friends, no peace, only grumpy George and the gloomy prospect of COVID and more lockdowns.

Frank stood there clinging to her, unable to say anything, not willing to let her go.

"Promise me you will come back, Frank," Fiona managed to whisper.

He didn't remember getting on the plane, only that he finally managed to stop shaking when the flight attendant sat him down and the plane finally started moving.

Chapter 35

For someone who hated flying, an eight-seater commuter plane was a challenging experience. Cramped conditions on the tiny aircraft, with the seats squashed together and no aisle down which to escape, made Kevin feel claustrophobic, and the presence of the pilot less than a few feet away made him anxious. It hadn't helped that he had spent most of the day in a bad mood, fed up with Frank avoiding him and everyone seemingly oblivious to the fact that he, not Frank, had paid for the whole trip. Even the news that Frank was going to meet Kevin separately at the airport had been relayed to him by Jack.

But his mood had lifted the moment he saw Frank approaching the aircraft a few minutes earlier. He looked like a broken man, hardly able to stand as a stewardess escorted him towards the red and blue plane. As Frank sat down a few seats behind him, Kevin felt ready for forgiveness, finally able to understand that Frank was not a bad person, merely a casualty of war, someone who had been to hell and back.

As the plane began its sprint down the runway, he gripped the side of his seat in anticipation. Soon they would be at the main airport and his time on these islands would end. The trip had not answered the questions about his father's disappearance, but walking in his father's footsteps had changed his outlook on life. He had knocked down a few barriers that had stopped him from moving on. One day, he would return. He was still young. He would be better prepared next time, do things properly. He would visit the places that he had been unable to this time, San Carlos and Fitzroy. Except next time, he would not go with Frank but with his wife and daughter.

For the first time in years, his life seemed uncluttered. The last few years of COVID and separation had unsettled him, but now he realised that he had never been able to appreciate what he had, that he had never stopped to smell the roses. Now he had a new goal—to work on his marriage, refill the coffers and salvage what he could before it was too late.

He smiled with relief as the plane took off. As the plane flew higher into the sky, he smiled at the spectacular view of Port Stanley on his left. From up here, it looked like a little village, a small concentration of little Lego bricks amidst a mass of water and treeless land. Next time he returned, perhaps the vast stretches of empty sea would once again be filled with cruise ships.

For so long these islands had meant nothing to him, just a pile of rocks on the other side of the world. Bleak, cold, and barren wasteland eight thousand miles from home, but now, as he looked down, he saw them in a different light. For the people who lived here, these islands were where they'd been born, where they lived, loved, married, and died. These islands were the islands their ancestors had lived on, the location of the graves of their parents and fore-fathers, their churches. These islands were their childhood and their old age; their stories entwined with the beaches, coves, mountains, and streams; the houses and the settlements and the town that they gave names to. These islands were their home.

As the famous mounds of Two Sisters, Mount Tumbledown, and Mount Longdon came into view, he gasped at the realisation that down to his immediate left was Wireless Ridge. It looked so peaceful, yet down there was, amongst the jagged rock and stone, where the conflict had finally come to an end, where bombs and mortars and shrapnel had once rained down, where soldiers had been mortally wounded and where many people had lost their lives. Down there was where Frank had had a mental breakdown that had, in turn, had a huge effect on his own life.

As the plane started to glide left, he could have sworn he saw a flash coming from near the top of the ridge. A flashing light that twinkled like a kind of metal, but he thought nothing more of it. Instead, he smiled and closed his eyes, feeling peace he had not felt for a long time.

Chapter 36

As the plane began its journey to Chile, Frank felt a little calmer. Unlike the cramped flight to Mount Pleasant, this plane was more spacious and quieter. At first, he believed the presence of his new necklace was making him feel better, but after a while he realised it was because of the comfort of having his new phone in his hand.

He found it ironic that the technology he had hated for so many years had now become so essential to his survival. He had always found them an unnatural intrusion, startling and noisy, shaking his head in puzzlement at the younger generation's slavery to the devices. But now he understood. Thanks to his new phone, he would never be alone. Fiona would always be on the other end, reminding him that wherever he was, she was never far away, that he was not alone.

After landing at Mount Pleasant, there had been a long wait before getting on the next plane and he had managed to have a quick FaceTime with Fiona. He had even chatted to Kevin, who had been kind enough to help get his new present from Fiona working, some Bluetooth AirPods. He'd been pleased to find out they were a lot simpler to work than he had anticipated, that technology had made so many leaps and bounds.

As he calmly looked out of the plane window, he knew there were many challenges ahead. The world was in an uncertain, perilous state and COVID was not going away. Who knew what the future held or if he could manage to get back here if his health took a turn for the worse.

Most of all, what would happen to the nightmares? He hadn't had one for a while, but he prayed if they returned, he would have the strength to dismiss them, to understand they were harmless. Afterall, he had achieved so much, learnt more about himself in the last few weeks than his whole life. The trip had finally given him closure. Yes, he would never know what happened to Baz, but he had finally made his peace with it. Fiona had shown him there were other ways forward.

And Kevin? This trip had been a meaningful one for him too. He looked over to his left, where he sat next to him on the same row. He had his headphones on, his eyes closed, and yet he still looked sad. It seemed ironic that after the drama, the trip had brought them closer together. He felt sorry for the lad—the trip had not given him the answers he had wanted for sure, but he was still young. Maybe one day he would find out what had happened to his father.

Feeling emotional, he tapped Kevin on the shoulder to get his attention.

Kevin smiled and took off his headphones.

"Kevin, I just wanted to say thank you," Frank said.

"What do you mean?" Kevin said, looking surprised.

"I mean, thanks for all you tried to do, for taking me with you and all that."

"You're welcome, Frank," Kevin said, still eying him suspiciously.

"I'm sorry too that I've sort of neglected you the last week. You know, it's been..."

"Don't be sorry, Frank. I understand."

"I know it's not been what I expected, but I've learnt to move on and count my blessings."

"How do you mean, Frank?"

"Do you know that 'Ryan' movie, Kev?"

"Ryan movie?"

"The Spielberg film?"

"You mean 'Saving Private Ryan?' "

"Yeah, that's the one."

"Yes, I remember it. Why?"

"I was thinking about it recently. It's a good way to explain how I feel sometimes. That guy, Matt Damon, when Tom Hanks dies at the end of the film, it's survivor's guilt he feels."

"How do you mean?"

"When Hanks says 'earn this'—well, that's how I feel about the promise I made to your dad. It's how I feel when I think of all those who didn't come home. I came home, they didn't. I have failed. I haven't earned it. That's why I haven't enjoyed my life since."

"Frank, don't be so hard on yourself?" Kevin said, turning his attention back to his phone.

Frank suddenly felt tired, the sleeping pill he had taken ten minutes earlier now starting to work. Then he noticed Fiona had sent him a new text message.

"Hi, Frank, hopefully by now you have your AirPods working and you have the noise cancellation mode on. This is a link to the song you told me about, 'Tunnel of Love' by Dire Straits. All you have to do is click on the link and you will begin to hear the song. When you listen to it, remember that I love you, Frank."

He checked that his AirPods were on noise cancellation as Kevin had patiently shown him earlier and then clicked on the link. It took him to some app called Spotify and then almost immediately music started playing. It was a special shorter version of the eight-minute song called 'Tunnel of Love Part 2,' and soon he was listening to the croaky voice of Mark Knopfler singing about carousels, carnival arcades, palisades, Cullercoats and Whitley Bay.

It had been so long since he'd heard this song, but now it was being fed directly, he was astounded by the clarity of sound, the sensuous joy of hearing beautiful music.

For him, the song was a memory of the past, when he was twelve years old, when life was good. When he was happy and carefree, when innocence was all the rage, when life was simple and straightforward. When the purity of his existence had yet to be unspoiled by the depravity of adulthood. No evil, no war, no death.

It was also, as the slow, melodic sound of the guitar solo began, a song of loss. Finally, his body seemed to give way and he heaved, unable to stop shaking uncontrollably. The tears came, and just as he feared, he could not stop. His thoughts flashed back to his happy childhood. Newcastle, the smell of home. It might have ended abruptly when they moved, but inside his heart, the memories were still there. Just like his love for Fiona, nothing, not even war or trauma, could ever take them away.

Luckily, by the time Knopfler's emotional tugging of the heartstrings ended, the sleeping pill had fully kicked in and he started to drift into sleep.

Straight away, he could almost feel a new dream coming, his subconscious talking to him. What had triggered it? Was it the emotional music, the buzz of background jet motors, or simply the peace he felt inside. Whatever dream was about to unfold, it was, he told himself that his mind was ready, that there was nothing to fear.

As the dream began, it immediately felt different. Having spent so many months dreaming about the hill at Darwin and the rock or the SS *Uganda*, the change of surroundings was a shock. He was not on the battlefield, no longer being fired at, not on some ship, but running down a brown, soggy hill. Out of breath, he looked to his right and saw many others were running down too with him. Though he was exhausted, the adrenaline kept him going. He knew he had to get to his destination because lives depended on it.

In the far distance, out on the sea, he saw the *Galahad* beneath huge plumes of black smoke. Arriving at the bottom of the hill, he found himself right next to the sea as small lifeboats with survivors started reaching the shore. There was a lot of shouting and screaming as a mass of people helped pull the lifeboats in on a rope, like a game of tug of war. As the lifeboat finally moored and the survivors staggered ashore, Frank noticed a lot of the people were burnt and screaming in pain, some of their clothes seemed to have melted and their skin had been cut to ribbons. He was desperate to help, but as he stood there gaping in shock at the survivors, he felt so redundant. His brief medical training had not covered how to treat burns and there was not much he could do.

In the near distance, he saw one victim lying on the beach, waiting for medical attention, and he ran towards him. He knelt and checked his pulse. As he waited, he could see the livid scar on his wrist where the metal of his Army-issue watch had burned into the skin. He got ready to offer words of comfort as he administered the syrette of morphine he had taken from his own beret. He looked down at the charred swollen face and gasped.

It was Baz Turner.

Baz looked puzzled at first, as if shocked that Frank was there, unable to imagine what sequence of events had led him to this bay. He noticed Baz trying to say something and leaned over to listen to his whispers.

"Find the rock, Frank!" he snarled sarcastically before bursting into hysterics.

Frank put his fingers in his ears, trying to block the evil laugh, but before he could do so, there was a big white flash followed by an explosion that covered him in a red mist.

He opened his eyes to find Kevin looking over him, tapping him on his arm, looking concerned.

"Frank? Frank? Are you okay?"

Taking a moment to remember where he was, he smiled. The nightmare hadn't hurt him. He was drenched in sweat, but he was no longer overcome with panic, the stench of gunpowder and death no longer made him nauseous.

He looked at Kevin and smiled. "I'm fine, Kev. It was nothing, just another silly dream."

Chapter 37

EPILOGUE

Olivia Short stood by the window in her fourth-floor office, neatly placing her right forefinger and thumb into the white interior shutters to create a little space from which to peek outside. The location of her office was one of the perks of working for the Ministry of Defence—right in the heart of central London, home to iconic landmarks like the Houses of Parliament, Big Ben, and the London Eye and Westminster. Omicron still lingered over the city so the crowds outside were noticeably lighter and having spent so much of the last few years working from home, the views were always a welcome relief.

Reluctantly, she closed the gap and walked back to her desk. Soon it would be time for lunch, and she still had some work to do. Final decisions were needed on two requests for information concerning individuals who had fought in the Falklands War of 1982. As she clicked on the relevant secret files on her computer, she acknowledged she knew little about this conflict except that it was infamous for its veil of secrecy. Media coverage was heavily censored, conveniently aided by limited broadcasting technology that meant most television coverage was often delayed by weeks. This helped to explain why so much information never emerged until years after the conflict was over.

Both requests today were concerning the Freedom of Information Act, an act originally formed to facilitate an open and transparent public administration, but in practice, especially when it came to military matters, the weight of importance given to public interest was much lighter. Not only could certain information potentially compromise the country's security but it could also cause huge distress to relatives of the informants or victims.

As she opened the first email request that had been forwarded to her office, she sighed. This particular record must have been sent to her in error. It was asking for the release of military records for Private Frank Drysdale. More specifically, the request concerned revealing the circumstances on how the person in question had obtained his shot wounds at the battle of Wireless Ridge on June 13th, 1982. As Mr. Drysdale was still living, the act did not allow access to their own personal data such as their health records or credit reference file. Only Mr. Drysdale could request that kind of information and through another department. However, despite the erroneous request, she was curious why someone had requested the information and opened the secret file. It didn't take her long to find the controversial part of the record.

> Some time after witnessing the sinking of the *Sir Galahad* and participating in the rescue of those onboard, Private Drysdale suffered a nervous breakdown. It is believed that as the battle of Wireless Ridge ended, he tried to

kill himself by shooting himself with a stolen enemy pistol. As he was considered mentally unstable, it was decided to place him under supervision on board the SS *Uganda* where he was also treated for his shoulder injury. In order not to distract from the just announced Allied victory, he was medically discharged and sent home to be treated in Woolwich Mental Hospital where he remained a patient for three months.

She sighed, unwilling to read more, reminded again of the unseen tragedy of war. Back in 1982, not much was known about trauma and mental illness. Most sufferers of trauma were never diagnosed because help was either refused or never sought out in the first place. However, it was an easy decision. She closed the file and clicked the Reject box on the request.

She then opened the second email. Strangely it was from the same lawyer as the first request. He was seeking more information on Baz Turner, a member of 2 PARA, whose death was listed as Missing in Action. The lawyer claimed that under Section 62 of the Act, any information regarding Baz Turner was now a "historical record" and could therefore be released.

She scrolled down the computer screen until she found the relevant secret report and started to read.

It is considered highly probable that Baz Turner was killed by a phosphorus grenade thrown by an enemy soldier who managed to avoid capture and escape back to Port Stanley. Unfortunately, because of the chaos that ensued from the war ending and the need to enter the capital to ensure a sensible surrender, correct protocols were not followed.

After careful consideration, the decision was made to cover up this information for three reasons. Firstly, further investigation of the alleged body was hampered by the fact that the battlefield area in question was still mined. Secondly, no dog tags were found, despite repeated attempts to search for them. Thirdly, and most importantly, even after mine clearance, the body was never found.

She nodded in agreement. It was one of the sad aspects of war that bodies could be destroyed, burned, or buried by the type of high-explosive munitions routinely used in modern warfare. Curious, she continued to read.

Private Turner had quickly recovered from a shrapnel injury and was keen to rejoin his battalion after treatment at Ajax Bay. However, because of unforeseen factors that delayed his return, most notably the sinking of the *Sir Galahad*, he was only able to join the battle of Wireless Ridge an hour after it had started, explaining why most of the battalion had not seen him or known he was there.

She thought of the poor families who never got the peace of knowing how their loved ones died. Perhaps the outcome of this particular case might had been different if DNA testing had been available. However, she had to agree with the assessment. With no body and no identification, the MIA classification was correct. However unfair it seemed that a deceased's family could not access information that might shed more light on the circumstances of his disappearance, the guidelines given to her were clear and it was not her job to question the morality of these matters.

She moved her mouse and clicked on Reject.

As she got up from her desk, she thought it an odd coincidence that both the requests she had just rejected were indirectly linked to the same battle, Wireless Ridge. It was very unusual to get a request from a forty-year-old conflict, let alone two from the same battle.

Who knows, perhaps they were related in some way.

She looked impatiently at her watch and then turned off the computer and went to lunch.

Chapter 38

As Ronald Johnson walked down the north side of Wireless Ridge, he marvelled at the spectacular view of Port Stanley. It reminded him of the Scottish Highlands they had visited a few years earlier. It looked so small from up here, their presence so insignificant amidst such a huge mass of sea and land. As the winds threatened to blow him over, he felt relieved he had brought a spare winter jacket. The weather was always unpredictable in the month of May, especially when you were this high up on the top of ridges, but even he had been surprised by the ferocity of the gale force winds blowing today.

Now retired, his love was military history and he and his wife Barbara had always been fascinated by war. They loved nothing better than to scour old battlefields, looking not only for trenches or artillery craters but also personal items, cooking stands made from fencing wire, cut up oil drums for metal sheeting to construct shelters, bullets and bomb fragments. Anything that might tie the nature to the battlefield and help understand better what happened in the conflict.

How different it was from their last visit to the islands four years earlier. Back then, they had arrived in December, the official Falkland Islands tourist season, and the weather had been a little friendlier. There had also been more tourists and, having spent a week visiting the usual tourists' sights, this time around they wanted to do something a little more challenging. A crew member on the cruise boat had suggested a trip up Wireless Ridge, one of the lesser-known battles of the conflict.

Today the goal had been to get to the top of the ridge with the help of a 4 X 4 and then head down the other side, northwards, following the path down to where 2 PARA had started the battle. The trip today was a little more special because a lot of stuff had happened since their last trip. Covid had wreaked its havoc on the world, and their Antarctic cruise had been cancelled a few times. Now that there was no longer a requirement to quarantine in the islands, their life of travel resumed.

They had only descended about twenty metres when he heard Barbara screaming to his right. Such was the abundant foundations of twisted rocks, it took him a few minutes to reach her.

"What is it, love? What have you found," he managed to say as he approached her out of breath, wishing he were a few years younger.

"Ron, look!"

His eyesight was not as good as his wife's, but as he looked closer, he made out what looked like a piece of chain or something. It twinkled in the reflection of the sun, and so his first reaction was that some tourist had dropped it, but, on closer inspection, he saw it was covered in rust and dirt and concluded that its appearance could only be explained by forty years of exposure to the ridge's harsh climate.

"What is it, Barbara?" he asked, hoping his wife had a better idea.

"Looks like some sort of necklace, I think."

"Where did you find it?"

"I was looking for bullet cases in this rock and found this in one of the holes."

As he took the object and examined it closer, he noticed there was some kind of engraving on it. He tried to rub off the mud and rust with his glove.

"It says something, Barbara," he said, reaching for the reading glasses in his jacket pocket.

"What does it say, Ronald? Read it, read it aloud," she said in an excited manner.

"No, it doesn't make any sense."

"Baz? I think. Ang? I think it's Spanish."

"Spanish?"

"Yeah, that's the Argentinian language?"

"It's burned and half the necklace seems to have been torn off or something. It probably belonged to one of the Argentinian soldiers."

Disappointed at not being able to understand the engraving, he placed the necklace on the nearest rock and took a photo with his mobile. He then picked it up and handed it back to his wife. He had always tried to show respect to the soldiers who had lost their lives on the battlefield. This was obviously a personal item best left alone, very different from the usual bullet fragments they typically found. It felt wrong to take it.

"Put it back where you found it, Barbara," he said and then they continued their trek down the ridge.